Praise for Kerry Barrett

'Strong characters, addictive dialogue and an absorbing story. This book is a runaway success'

'Absolutely loved this book! Finished it in two sittings! An enchanting read'

'Fantastic debut novel'

'A really terrific read'

'Sprinkled with magic and full of humour'

'Great witchy fun'

'I was under a spell . . . I could relate to the characters as if they were my friends . . . I loved it. Well done, Kerry'

'Fantastic read . . . I was looking for a book that would be the perfect read for my holidays and this really hit the mark'

'The storyline had a good number of twists and turns to keep you going and the ending was great'

'Perfect with a cup of hot chocolate on a rainy day'

'I thoroughly enjoyed Kerry Barrett's debut novel even though not my usual type of book. The characters were engaging from the first page and the story flowed really well'

KERRY BARRETT was a bookworm from a very early age and did a degree in English Literature, then trained as a journalist, writing about everything from pub grub to *EastEnders*. Her first novel, *Like a Charm*, took six years to finish and was mostly written in longhand on her commute to work, giving her a very good reason to buy beautiful notebooks. Kerry lives in London with her husband and two sons, and Noel Streatfeild's *Ballet Shoes* is still her favourite novel.

Also by Kerry Barrett

Like a Charm

KERRY BARRETT

ONE PLACE. MANY STORIES

HQ
An imprint of HarperCollins*Publishers* Ltd
1 London Bridge Street
London SE1 9GF

www.harpercollins.co.uk

HarperCollins*Publishers*
Macken House, 39/40 Mayor Street Upper,
Dublin 1 D01 C9W8

This paperback edition 2023

2

First published in Great Britain as *Bewitched, Bothered and Bewildered* by HQ,
an imprint of HarperCollins*Publishers* Ltd 2013

Copyright © Kerry Barrett 2013

Kerry Barrett asserts the moral right to be
identified as the author of this work.
A catalogue record for this book is
available from the British Library.

ISBN: 9780008653743

MIX
Paper | Supporting
responsible forestry
FSC™ C007454

This book is produced from independently certified FSC™ paper
to ensure responsible forest management.

For more information visit: www.harpercollins.co.uk/green

Printed and Bound in the UK using
100% Renewable Electricity at CPI Group (UK) Ltd

For my boys, big and small.

I was comple

bar stool, legs

Harry for ins

'Seven o'cl   ...... wnarr, she'd said
in her message. 'Don't be late. It's important.'

She was passing through town, she'd said, flying into Heathrow
from the States and back to Scotland from City. Bad planning
on her part. And even worse planning on mine to work spit-
ting distance from the bar she'd chosen. I'd briefly considered
changing jobs to get out of meeting her, but even I could see
that was a bit extreme.

And so, here I was. With my legs uncomfortably wrapped
around the chrome legs of a shiny stool, and my elbow in a puddle
of something, in a bar full of the City types I spent a lot of time
avoiding. And – I squinted at my watch in the dim light – it was
now 7.25pm and there was still no sign of Harry.

I shifted awkwardly on my perch and tried once more to get
the barman's attention. He'd been ignoring me since I arrived,
despite my best attempts at eye contact.

Finally, I thought, as his gaze shifted in my direction. But
no, instead he served the woman standing behind me, who had

glossy hair and the kind of honey-coloured skin that comes from a lifetime of winters spent abroad.

That did it. I moved my arm out of the puddle, rested my wrist on the cold bar and waggled my fingers, gently, in the direction of the barman. A small shower of pink sparks – nothing anyone would notice – wafted from my fingertips. The barman looked puzzled for a moment, then he picked a bottle of Pinot Grigio from the fridge, dropped it into an ice bucket and presented it to me, along with two glasses, with a flourish.

'Nice,' said a voice in my ear. 'And you didn't even have to ask.'

'Hello, Harry,' I said. Of course she would choose that moment to arrive. She didn't kiss me. Instead, she leaned over, scooped up the wine bucket and tilted her head in the direction of a booth.

I was expected to follow, clearly. I picked up the glasses, then had to put them down again so I could slide off the barstool without mishap. I resisted the temptation to turn around and descend backwards, but only just. Then I picked up the glasses again and trotted after my cousin, just like I'd been trotting after her my whole life.

As I approached the table she'd chosen, I noticed her normally immaculately made-up face was pale, with dark rings under her eyes. And her slouchy cashmere sweater hung off her. She grabbed the glass I offered, glugged wine into it and drained it. I felt slightly uneasy. Harry being in control was one of the constants in my life.

'What's the matter?' I asked as I shuffled sideways along the seat into the booth.

Harry waited for me to sit, then pushed a glass in my direction.

'It's Mum,' she said in her typically forthright way. 'She's got breast cancer.'

I put my hand to my mouth in shock.

'Oh God,' I said. 'Poor Auntie Suky.'

Harry took another swig of her wine.

'She should be OK because they seem to have caught it early enough. But she's in for a rough few months.'

She looked at me. 'You have to go,' she said.

I was already shaking my head.

'No,' I said. 'Absolutely not.'

'My mum needs you,' Harry said.

'You go.' I tipped my wine into my mouth and poured another glass. 'She's your mum.'

Harry looked away. I thought for a moment she had tears in her eyes, but perhaps it was just the light in the bar.

'I've got some stuff going on at the moment, Esme,' she said. 'I can't leave work just now. I'll come as soon as I can.'

'I don't care. I'm not going.'

I was annoyed she'd even asked. Going to see Suky meant seeing my own mum, and Harry knew how shaky my relationship was with her.

'I know you're annoyed I even asked,' she said.

'Don't do that.' I scowled at her. I hated when she poked about in my head and read my mind.

'What?' she said, her pretty face full of innocence.

Infuriated, I shook my head again. Harry ignored me.

'I spoke to your mum,' she said. I felt a flash of anger that she'd spoken to Mum when I hadn't. 'She says there's been a bit of trouble.'

'What kind of trouble?'

'A few things have gone wrong at the café.'

I shrugged.

'There's nothing I can do about that.' My career as a lawyer was far away from my family's quaint tearoom.

Harry caught my fingers and squeezed them.

'You can help,' she said. 'You have to help. You know I'd be there if I could – it's just really tricky for me at the moment.'

'I don't do witch stuff anymore,' I said.

Harry arched her perfectly plucked eyebrows.

'Then what was that at the bar?'

She had a point. What I'd done at the bar –and what she'd done when she echoed my thoughts back to me – was witchcraft. Because, though I denied it and ignored it, I was a witch. Harry was one too. And so were our mums. And our gran before them. You know how it goes.

But a long time ago, I'd turned my back on my mum and witchcraft, and now I only ever used it secretly, quietly and – often pretty badly – to make everyday life a bit easier. If I needed a parking space, one would open up. A mess in my kitchen? No problem. Couldn't find the remote control? It would just appear like – well, like magic. Anything more complicated though, and it didn't always go as smoothly as I'd liked, so I tended to avoid pushing my luck when it came to spells. It was a strategy that worked for me and I had no intention of that changing any time soon.

'I'll come up as soon as I can,' Harry was saying. 'Next week, probably. Your mum needs you, Ez. My mum needs you. I . . .'

There was a pause. I looked at her in expectation. But apparently she'd finished.

I pushed my glass of wine away and picked up my bag.

'Sorry,' I said, shuffling back along the bench. 'I have to go back to the office. Don't you have a plane to catch?'

Chapter 2

'I told her, there was absolutely no way I was going,' I said to Dom, my sort-of-boyfriend later that evening. I'd bumped into him when I'd gone back to the office to pick up my things, and persuaded him to come back to mine, which hardly ever happened. He looked out of place in my tiny flat; too big and too male as he lounged against my Cath Kidston cushions and smiled at me as I ranted and paced the floor in front of him.

'Absolutely no way,' I repeated.

Dom looked at me, a glint of mischief in his brown eyes.

'So when are you leaving?

I screwed up my nose.

'Tomorrow,' I said miserably. 'Straight after work.'

He chuckled, but to give him his due, he didn't labour the point. Instead he patted the cushion next to him and pulled me down on to the sofa. I cuddled into him, enjoying the rare pleasure of having him all to myself.

'I'm in court all day tomorrow,' he said. 'So I won't get to see you before you go.'

'Well, we'd better make tonight count then,' I said, looking up at him in what I hoped was a coquettish, flirty manner.

Dom leaned down to kiss me, when suddenly his phone rang,

making me jump and ruining the moment. I glared at him as he answered and motioned for me to be quiet.

'Hello, Rebecca,' he said. 'Yep, got stuck in the office, but I'm just finishing up here.'

I pulled my legs away from Dom, stood up and flounced into my tiny kitchen where I slumped against the work surface. Rebecca was the reason Dom was only my 'sort-of boyfriend'. Because she was sort of his wife. Well, if I was being honest, there was no sort of about it. She was his actual wife. Which made me his actual mistress.

I wasn't proud of myself. I knew what I was doing was wrong. But Dom had charmed me and I felt as though I had no control over my actions. He'd broken through all my defences. And actually, the secrecy and the subterfuge suited me quite well.

Dom and I had been working together for two years. We'd been sleeping together for nearly a year. The first time it happened I'd been working late in the office, desperate to make my mark in a company full of overachievers. As I pored over files and wrote reams of notes, Dom appeared at my office door.

'Come for a drink,' he said.

'I can't,' I replied, not even looking up. Dom had been circling me for weeks, months even, flirting and going out of his way to pay me attention. I wasn't interested. I avoided relationships and preferred to spend all my spare time working.

'You work too hard.' He walked towards my desk and sat down on the chair in front of me.

'So do you.' I turned a page in the folder I was reading and carried on making notes in the margin.

'Pleeeease,' Dom whined like a little boy. 'I'm sooooo bored.'

In spite of myself I laughed and finally looked up. His wide eyes with a hint of mischief met mine, and a tiny bud of lust curled in my stomach. How could I resist?

'I can't go for a drink,' I said firmly. 'But if you go and get me a coffee, I'll take a break and we can chat for five minutes.'

Dom had brought me a coffee – and a bottle of wine – and we chatted for hours that night. And the next night, when we both worked late again. And after a few 'dates' in the office, we went out for dinner. Just an above-board business dinner between colleagues at a restaurant near work.

Except the restaurant was expensive and softly lit and we didn't talk about business.

When we finally staggered out into the street, dizzy with red wine, good food and lust, I raised my arm to hail a cab. Dom caught my hand and pulled me to face him.

'What now?' he asked. His face was close to mine and I could feel his breath on my lips. My legs were like jelly and although I knew I should pull away, I couldn't.

'You're married,' I whispered.

Dom shook his head.

'Only on paper,' he assured me. 'Not for much longer.' A flicker of something – guilt? – crossed his eyes.

'The ball's in your court, Esme,' he said, pulling me closer.

I opened my mouth to tell him to go home to his wife. But instead I found myself leaning forward to kiss him. He tasted of garlic and coffee and fun and I was bewitched.

So when a taxi pulled up beside us and Dom got in with me, and gave the cabbie my address, I didn't protest. And that was that.

A year of snatched meetings, illicit evenings and "it's complicated" excuses when I asked about his divorce, Dom was still married and I still felt terrible whenever I thought of his wife. And I still hated it if she called when I was with him.

It was good this way, I told myself. I was happy working long hours and spending time alone in my flat or at the gym. Having a full-time boyfriend would cramp my style. Plus, it suited me to have some distance between us. I may not have been an enthusiastic user of magic, but all my family were. Just the thought of inviting a boyfriend home and watching his face as Mum made Sunday dinner in her own special way gave me chills. And my family's track record when it came to my love life was not good. But still my heart ached when Dom slipped out of my bed at night and went home to his wife.

I ignored the nagging voice inside me that told me what I was doing was wrong, and the suspicion that Dom wasn't being entirely honest about his divorce. I ignored my guilt about Rebecca, and, most of all, I ignored the feeling that despite my fabulous, well-paid job, my gorgeous flat and my handsome, sophisticated sort-of boyfriend, I was lonely.

'I'm going to miss you.' Dom interrupted my thoughts. He had finished his phone call and come to find me in the kitchen. He snaked his arms round my waist and planted a kiss on my neck.

'No you won't,' I said, pulling his arms off me. 'You won't even notice I'm not here.'

Dom winked at me. 'Of course I will. I love you,' he said. I gaped at him. He'd never said that before. Ignoring my silence, Dom picked up his car keys.

'Bye,' he called from the hall, as he blew me a kiss.

I pretended to catch it. 'Bye then,' I whispered.

Chapter 3

The next day at work was frantic. My boss, Maggie, almost tipped me over the edge because she was frantically preparing for a meeting with another Hollywood couple about the baby they were trying to adopt, and she couldn't decide what to wear. I was trying very hard to tie up any loose ends and pass on the cases that I could before I went to Scotland. And I was wrestling with a client who'd decided to start Tweeting vindictive messages to her cheating husband despite my desperate voicemails begging her to stop.

I was a family lawyer. It sounded quite fluffy but it wasn't. In my experience, family law was about as nasty as it gets. Especially the bit I was involved with. Think cheating Premiership foot-ballers, wronged pop stars and vicious custody battles, and you'd be pretty close. Still, it was a living. And it kept me very, very busy, which was the idea.

Eventually, things calmed down enough for me to sit back in my chair and look at my phone. I knew I had to phone Mum and tell her I was coming up. Harry had emailed to say she'd passed on my flight details, but if I was expecting to stay it was only polite to call. It wasn't like Mum and I never talked. We did, of course. But we weren't mates; not close like Harry and Suky were. I would never tell her about Dom, for example, or really fill her in on anything happening in my life – because the last time I did, when I was sixteen, it all backfired on me in the worst way and Mum and I had a major falling out. Major.

To be honest, it had been brewing for years. I was a shy, clumsy teenager whose desperation to fit in clashed – badly – with my family's bohemian side. But until the big drama, we'd all rubbed along pretty well. Harry was ten years older than me and thick as thieves with Suky, who'd had her when she was barely out of her teens herself. Back then I adored Harry – whose real name was Harmony. She was beautiful, funny, clever – still was, I supposed – and amazingly talented in the witchcraft department. She'd long since left home and was living in Edinburgh, but we still saw a lot of her.

My mum – who was Suky's twin sister – and I were less close but we still got on – pretty much. We weren't as close as Harry and Suky, who were more like friends than mother and daughter, but we did ok. And unlike many teenagers, I also got on with my dad, who'd split up with Mum before I was born and now had a glamorous wife and two little boys.

As for the cause of the rift, I won't bore you with all the sorry details, but imagine a spiky teenager who had fallen in love for the first time and a mum who – in some misguided attempt to make us as close as Suky and Harry – decided to meddle.

After the sparks had stopped flying (and I meant literally of course) I fled. I took off to Edinburgh, to my big cousin who would make everything OK. Except she didn't. She sat me in the kitchen of her tiny top-floor flat in Leith and listened as I poured my heart out. And then do you know what she did? She laughed. She laughed and told me not to take myself so seriously. In short, she took my already fragile heart and shattered it into a thousand pieces.

That was that really. Luckily Dad came to my rescue with an offer of paying for me to do A Levels at a school near where he lived in Cheltenham. I packed my bags, moved to England and never looked back. Until now.

Nerves jangling, I looked at the phone on my desk. Then I grabbed it and dialled Mum's number before I had a chance to change my mind.

'It's me,' I said when she answered. There was a brief silence and then I heard her breathe out, almost in relief.

'Esme, darling,' she said. I immediately felt guilty at how pleased she was to hear from me.

'Harry said you're coming.'

'I'm coming,' I told her. I bit my lip. 'Is that going to be OK?'

'Of course it is,' she said. I could almost feel her smiling down the line. 'It'll be good to see you.'

Maggie appeared in the door of my office holding up two blouses. I pointed to the one on her left, knowing she'd wear the other one.

I knew Mum wanted me to say it would be good to see her too, but I just couldn't lie. Instead, I asked her about Suky and told her when to expect me. And I was relieved when my phone beeped to tell me I had another call, and I could say goodbye.

As I tried to talk my vindictive client out of emailing indiscreet pictures of her philandering husband to all the contacts in his address book, my assistant Chrissie stuck her head and an arm round my door and put a large latte on my bookshelf. She gave me a quick, sympathetic smile and I wondered how much of my phone call to Mum she'd heard (or listened to, more like).

I stared at my coffee, lacking the energy to walk over and pick it up. Then I checked Chrissie wasn't lurking outside, and gently waggled my fingers in the direction of my cup. In a shower of pink sparks the latte flew across my office. It landed neatly on a pile of papers and a drip plopped onto a super injunction I'd been preparing for a TV presenter. I wiped it off with a tissue, thinking that coffee spills were the least of my worries. The two halves of my life – two halves that I kept far, far apart – were coming together and I felt very uneasy.

Chapter 4

'We do have one car left,' the woman at the car hire desk told me much, much later. She tapped some keys on her computer and the printer began spewing out the reams of paper that I apparently needed to sign to hire a Nissan Micra.

I looked past her shoulder at the rain lashing the windows and sighed. Inverness never changed. Mindlessly I scribbled my signature on the many bits of paper the woman pushed towards me and tried to ignore the Tannoy that was announcing a flight to London. I'd be home soon, I told myself.

'It's a silver car,' the woman said, handing me the key. 'The registration number is on the fob and it's in space 60, row Z.' She gave a rueful chuckle. 'Oh dear, it's rather far away . . .'

Together we turned and looked at the rain streaming down the glass behind her. I was not traipsing past rows A to Y in this weather – for a Micra. I draped my jacket over my arm so it hid my hand, and wiggled my fingers. Her computer gave a loud beep.

'Oh I'm sorry,' she said. 'I've made a mistake. The only car we have left is a Mini – oh and it's in row A. That's lucky.'

'Isn't it?' I agreed. I took the new key she gave me and turned to leave with a self-satisfied smile. I tried not to listen as her computer beeped three times in a row and she banged the keyboard, cursing. My magic did sometimes backfire.

Despite my efforts, I was still wet by the time I reached the car. Muttering to myself under my breath and wiping a drip from the end of my nose, I hurled my sodden bags into the back seat and arranged my damp self in the driving seat. Craving a friendly voice, I scrabbled in my handbag for my mobile and turned it on, expecting a message from Dom after being on the plane. But my only message was from Maggie.

'Esme,' she shrieked. 'The meeting was just wonderful! It all went so well . . .'

I cut her message off, not interested in her gushing, then I flung my phone on to the passenger seat where it bounced once and disappeared down the side of the chair.

'Oh well, I'll find it later,' I thought. It wasn't as though Dom would be trying to get hold of me at this late hour. I expected he was spending the evening with Rebecca.

Of course I'd never met Rebecca but I had imagined every detail of her life with Dom. In fact, I'd imagined it twice. In the first scenario, Rebecca was pinched and thin-lipped. She never spoke to Dom except to say something negative and she never smiled.

In the second – the one I was currently torturing myself with – she was tall and beautiful with swishy hair and a stylish wardrobe. I imagined her and Dom spending weekends lounging around their fabulous Hampstead home – in truth, all I knew was they lived in North London somewhere – with their fabulous friends. Right now, they'd be spooning in their huge sleigh bed. I shuddered at the thought.

Pushing the image out of my head, I turned on the engine and drove out of the airport on to the main road. I was on my way and I was more than a little bit nervous. In fact, I was terrified.

Since I left home, I'd been very definitely in my Dad's camp. Not that he and Mum's separation – before I was even born – had been particularly acrimonious. They were just utterly mismatched.

My loyalty was with my dad, even though I loved my mum. Her witchiness, if that's even a word, was just too much for me.

My parents met back in the early 80s. Mum was in her late 20s. She'd come home for the summer, running from a doomed love affair in Glasgow, where she lived. Dad – a few years older, handsome in his RAF uniform – literally fell for her.

My mum had climbed one of the hills overlooking the village and was lying on the grass, planning what she was going to do with her life. Dad was on his way back to the RAF base a few miles away after a brisk jaunt up the slope – and he tripped over her. Not the most romantic meeting, but something about the woman with short white-blonde hair and big blue eyes won him over.

Needless to say, my mum's plans that day didn't include falling for a slightly conservative, very ambitious military man. And they definitely didn't include getting pregnant just a few months into their relationship. If she could have seen that far ahead (yes, I know some witches can do that, but our lot can't, more's the pity) I'm also sure she wouldn't have seen my dad sent off to the Kuwait before she'd even plucked up the courage to tell him she was pregnant. Or the injury that sent him behind a desk in a base in the Cotswolds.

Anyway, Mum was pregnant, lonely and living at home in the Highlands with her mum and Dad was miserable, nursing a gammy leg and readjusting to life after the war. It was never going to work. But to their credit they've never made me feel like I'd missed out. I lived with Mum and Gran, until she died when I was twelve, as well as Suky and Harry. I spent holidays with Dad – and later with his wife, Olivia, and their two boys. Olivia was posh and groomed and brilliantly clever and our relationship, while not wonderful, wasn't as terrible as it could be. She tolerated me and I tried not to annoy her too much. Or make a mess in her house.

Mum claimed she told Dad the truth about our family when she realised she was falling for him. Dad, though, didn't seem to know. I thought it was a bit like that cheesy Loch Ness film

– you remember? 'You have to believe before you can see'. And Dad just didn't believe. He joked about our 'lotions and potions' but as far as he was concerned, witchcraft was just a hobby.

The road was quiet as I drove north. Occasionally the lights of another car would blaze through the darkness, making me blink as they swept past, but for most of the time I was alone. I put on the radio but it interfered with my thoughts, so I switched it off again.

I squinted through the windscreen, trying to get my bearings in the lashing rain. Not much further. I felt sick with nerves and as I passed a sign for a B&B I had to use all my willpower not to turn off the road and spend the night.

I felt odd about going home after avoiding it for so long. My emotions were muddled and I veered from being nervous about seeing my family to looking forward to hearing all their news, and of course I was desperately worried about Suky. Mum had filled me in about her illness on the phone, but I'd never met anyone with cancer before. I didn't know what to expect and I was terrified of the unknown.

I could feel myself getting stressed as I thought about home, so I tried to put my worries aside and concentrate on driving. The weather was getting worse and the narrow roads weren't as familiar as they used to be.

Leaning forward in my seat, I drove carefully, peering through the rain and gloom, fearful I would hit a deer, until eventually, with my shoulders tense and a stiff neck, my headlights shone upon a large road sign.

Loch Claddach welcomes careful drivers, it proclaimed in tartan-edged, tourist-friendly glory. Breathing a sigh of relief, I jammed on the brakes and juddered to a halt underneath the garish sign. I was home.

I turned off the engine and sat in the car, listening to the rain drumming on the roof, while I tried to make sense of the way I was feeling. My head was pounding from the effort of driving and I was bursting with mixed emotions. I couldn't arrive in such a mess. I pulled my hairbrush from my bag and pulled my hair out of its twist, then I brushed it and pinned it up again, using my reflection in the windscreen in the dim light.

According to Mum, Suky had found a lump in her breast a month ago but went to the doctor's alone and kept quiet while she went for tests. Only when she was diagnosed did she come home and let her sister know what was happening.

'It was awful, Esme,' Mum had told me on the phone. 'We were having a glass of wine and talking about our day, just like normal. She said she'd had a tough day and then she just blurted it out. "Don't be upset," she said. How could I not be upset?'

That had been last week. Suky had already had an operation to remove her lump and she was now facing weeks of radiotherapy at the hospital in Inverness. I felt terrible for her and guilty that Mum or Harry hadn't called me straightaway.

I felt remote and detached from my family. But it wasn't surprising, I thought as I shoved my hairbrush back in my bag and gripped the steering wheel once more. I hardly ever came home. Occasionally, I'd fly in for Christmas, arriving on the 24th and leaving again on the 26th. One year I even got the sleeper and arrived on Christmas Day itself. The last time I'd been home was a few years ago now. I'd come up for a family reunion on Halloween, part of me hoping my attendance would be an olive branch that could rebuild my relationship with my mum. But it had been an unmitigated disaster. I'd felt hopelessly out of my depth among family members who looked vague and disappointed when I talked about my law degree and who conjured up cakes and entertainment at the drop of a (witch's) hat. When a great aunt – who hadn't managed to make the trip from her home in Australia – materialised in the living room, her flickery image like the recording of Princess Leia in *Star Wars*, I legged it. I faked a call from a neighbour, pretended a pipe had burst and ran for the airport. I realised it would be Halloween again in a couple of weeks. I sincerely hoped I would be safely back in London by then.

My mind was whirling from guilt to dread and back again as I sat in the cold car and looked at my old hometown though the rain. But most of all I was worried about Suky. Sweet, kind-hearted Suky, who sent me first letters, then emails after I'd left home, keeping me up to date with the family's news and making sure – in fact – that I was still part of the family. But she hadn't shared this news. I hadn't had so much as a hint.

I wiped the steamed-up windscreen with a gloved finger and peered out into the dreary night. I could see rows of darkened cottages, and beyond them, St Columba's church, with its spire lit up to impress the tourists. Not that there were likely to be many of them around on a cold October night.

Shivering, I turned the engine on again and turned the heater up to full. I drove forward and followed the road through town at a snail's pace. I knew I didn't need to drive that slowly, despite the weather, but somehow I couldn't make myself speed up. I didn't want to go home, I finally admitted to myself. I was too scared about what I might find there.

I shook my head, trying to dislodge the miserable thoughts that were stuck there, trod down the accelerator accidentally, and nearly drove the car up the pavement and into a post box. I grimaced.

'Get a grip,' I told myself out loud.

Clutching the steering wheel, I drove at a more sensible speed up the hill, past my old primary school and the neat little house where my headmistress still lived, and parked outside the house where I'd grown up.

Typically, while every other house in town was cloaked in darkness, ours blazed with light. I smiled, in spite of my misgivings, and turned off the engine. I took a deep breath, then I got out of the car and pulled my bags from the back seat. I stood still for a minute, determined to savour the silence before I went in.

Suddenly the front door flew open. My mother stood there, silhouetted against the bright hallway. I could see her short hair sticking up and she held a wine glass in one hand as she peered out into the darkness.

'Esme!' She sounded pleased. 'I thought it'd be you. Come in! Come away from the rain.'

Chapter 5

I stumbled across the gravel driveway, my bag banging against my legs. Mum tried to sweep me into a hug, but my bag and my stiff stance made it awkward. We stared at each other for a minute, then she grabbed my holdall, turned and led the way down the hall to the kitchen.

'How is she?' I asked. I wanted to perch on a stool like I used to when I'd come home from school and share my day with Mum while she cooked our tea, but I didn't. Instead, I hovered by the kitchen door like an uninvited guest.

Mum filled the kettle and paused to switch it on before she answered.

'She's not good,' she said quietly. 'She had her first radiotherapy session today and it seems to have knocked the stuffing out of her. But she'll be pleased to see you.' She nodded towards the living room. 'Why don't you go and say hello?'

Nervously I crept into the front room where Suky was asleep on the enormous squidgy sofa with a blanket over her legs. She looked pale and thin and it took me a huge effort not to gasp when I saw her.

Mum had followed me in from the kitchen and she put her hand on my shoulder gently.

'It's all happened so fast – she's exhausted,' she said. 'She's keeping her spirits up, though.'

I looked at my beautiful, lively aunt, hunched under a blanket like an old lady and rounded on Mum.

'Why can't you help her?' I hissed in a loud whisper. 'Isn't this what you *witches* do?'

Mum shook her head.

'You sound like Harry,' she said with a sad smile. 'She's been on the phone non-stop with theories she's found and spells to try. But messing with life and death is dangerous, Esme. That's not our sort of magic. We just have to help her the best we can.'

I shrugged. Magic was magic as far as I was concerned, and this house was full of it. It positively crackled through every room and hung around Mum like a force field. Harry was the aura reader in our family, but even my unpractised eye could see Suky's power was dim and wavery, like a candle about to burn out. It made me shiver with fear for her.

'I'll help,' I whispered to Mum, so as not to wake Suky. 'What can I do?'

Mum gestured with her head and I followed her back into the kitchen, closing the door behind me. I made for the kettle but Mum handed me a glass of wine instead.

'What can I do?' I repeated. Mum took a swig of wine and visibly braced herself.

'We need a Third,' she said.

I looked at her in horror. I'd been expecting to ferry Suky to appointments, do a supermarket run, maybe whip up a lasagne. I'd definitely not planned to become a vital cog in the coven's wheel.

Because a coven is basically what we had here. Witches, you see, were sociable souls. Obsessed with the number three. Oh, we could all do magic on our own, but for the really good stuff to happen, there needed to be three. Mum and Suky worked with a witch called Eva. She had wafted into Claddach on the day of my Granny's funeral and she'd been here ever since.

'Does Eva know you're asking me?' I said now.

Mum nodded.

'Yes,' she said. 'She thinks it would be better to have someone we know, rather than get in an agency witch.'

I gaped at her. Agency? Who knew witchcraft was so 21st century.

'What about Harry?' I managed to say.

'Harry's got some problems at work,' Mum said. 'I think it's worse than she's letting on, but she's not telling of course. I also think things may not be completely fine at home. But she's keeping quiet about that too. You know she'd be here if she could.'

I wasn't convinced. I knew Harry adored her mum, but she could be very selfish when she wanted to be. She used magic all the time. Seriously. All. The. Time. Which was why I thought she'd be so useful to Mum and Eva now. But if she wasn't helping then she wasn't helping – no one could make Harry do anything she didn't want to do, least of all me.

'We need you, Esme.' Mum held my hand tightly. 'Suky needs you.'

I sank down in a tatty armchair. They did need me, that much was true. They needed me to help in our family business – running the Claddach Café.

Mum, Suky and Eva ran the café together. Mum – who'd always been an amazing cook – did most of the baking but they all pitched in. Mum was also the business brain, so she did all the books. Eva, who was a talented potter and ceramicist, provided the crockery and in one corner, Suky had her 'pharmacy'. She had a comfy sofa, screened off from the café, and a shelf unit filled with an apothecary's dream of glass bottles. She offered a comforting ear and herbal remedies for the villagers' medical complaints. And for more, erm, *complicated* problems, and, of course, for those issues that hadn't quite been voiced, Mum and Eva were on hand to help.

It was an open secret that the McLeods could help with exam stress, fertility problems, annoying neighbours – anything really. Ask anyone outright and they'd laugh at you or dismiss Suky's remedies as a placebo. But in reality, just about everyone in

21

Claddach had a helping hand at one time or another, whether knowingly via Suky's potions, or unknowingly, thanks to Mum, Eva and Suky stirring secret spells into their cakes and lacing their biscuits with sorcery.

And like I said, that's why they needed me. The good stuff wouldn't really get going unless there were three of them casting the spell. With Suky ill, they needed me to make up the numbers and help them stir up the spells for their special cakes and bakes. They needed me to be the third member of their coven and it was absolutely, positively the last thing I wanted to do.

I looked at Suky, who was sleeping peacefully, her thin face showing no sign of pain. Then I looked at Mum who was watching me, waiting for my answer. Somehow I knew I'd regret what I was about to say.

'OK. I'll help out,' I said, shrugging my shoulders. I knew when I was beaten. 'But only a bit. I'm not getting mixed up in anything I shouldn't. I'll only help when we're asked to.'

Mum beamed at me, but I waved away her gushing thanks.

'It's late and I'm knackered,' I said. 'I'm off to my bed. We can talk about this tomorrow.'

I kissed Mum briefly and touched Suky's hand, then I climbed the stairs to my bedroom and pushed open the door. Turning on the light, I looked around. Mum hadn't redecorated since I'd left home and my walls were still sponged peach and cream. I'd thought it was the height of sophistication when I was fifteen. Now it just looked twee. My bed was made up with the Take That duvet cover I'd discarded as childish when I was fourteen. I was half annoyed and half touched that Mum had looked it out for me.

Knowing I'd regret it if I left it until the morning, I tugged my clothes out of my case and hung them up. My city clothes – I didn't really do casual – looked out of place in the old-fashioned wardrobe. Then I pulled on my pyjamas and sat on the edge of my bed. It was strange to be home after so long, but somehow it already felt like I'd never been away.

I picked up my phone and texted Dom, letting him know I'd arrived safely. I didn't expect a reply and I didn't get one, so I switched off the phone and put it on my bedside table. And then I noticed the book. It sat squarely next to my bed and I couldn't believe I hadn't noticed it before. Mind you, I thought to myself rolling my eyes, I couldn't be sure it had been there before. The book was about the size of a school exercise book but much thicker. It was bound in aged, brown leather and had no markings on the outside.

Picking it up I noticed someone – Mum no doubt – had stuck a piece of paper inside, with a smiley face drawn on it.

'Nice try, Mother,' I said out loud. I plumped my pillows up, then wriggled under my duvet and sat back with the unopened book in my lap. I had butterflies in my stomach and my hands were trembling. I didn't need to open it – I knew exactly what it was.

It was a spell book. All witches had them. They were heirlooms, passed down through families (mine had been left to me by my granny when she died. She left Harry an identical one; I suspected there was a stockpile somewhere) and they were supposed to be well cared for. It's implied, ridiculous as it sounded, that they were almost living things; a gateway to all sorts of magic, as well as a kind of logbook for successive witches to record their spells.

'Books are wonderful, Esme,' I remembered Mum telling me when I was small. 'But they can be dangerous. Why do you think the Nazis burned them? Spell books are even trickier to handle. Treat it like a wild animal.'

I'd gazed at her, wide-eyed.

'Will it bite me?' I'd asked.

Mum had laughed.

'Almost definitely not,' she said. But she hadn't looked very sure.

'Generations of McLeod witches have added to this book,' she said. 'The magic in here is very strong. Use it wisely and treat it with respect.'

With a flash of guilt I thought about how I'd actually treated it. I'd read it with Mum when I was a child, but when I hit my teens I'd cast it aside and abandoned it without a second thought when I'd left. Mum had clearly rescued it and kept it safe in case I ever needed it.

With shaking fingers I picked up the book. It was cold and hard. I turned it over in my hands and smoothed the cover, and as I did so, something strange happened. I felt – and I knew this sounded crazy – that the book recognised me. There was a sigh and suddenly the leather softened and warmed under my fingers.

Reassured and freaked out in equal measures, I opened the first page. Whatever I thought about my dubious inherited talents, I knew I had to brush up on my spells – even if I wasn't keen on being the Third. Apart from my magic being at best rusty and at worst unpredictable or even downright dangerous, I'd never agreed with my family's bad habit of interfering in people's lives without being asked – especially since I'd been on the receiving end of their meddling. But I knew the café couldn't survive without my help and I owed it to Suky to do whatever I could. Even if all I could do was make a few sparks and probably a bit of a mess.

So, even though I was apprehensive about facing my past, I decided to read my spell book and see how much I remembered. I blew the dust off the pages and settled down to read. Some of the pages were handwritten, some typed on an old-fashioned typewriter. Some had notes scribbled on them. There were even photos stuck in between some of the pages. It was fascinating, but it was late, and my eyes were soon heavy with sleep, so I put the book aside. I knew I had a lot of brushing up to do, but it could wait until morning. Realising I needed to get up again to switch off the light, I started to get out of bed, then, thoughtfully, I stopped.

'May as well start as I mean to go on,' I said to no one. And I waggled my fingers at the light instead. With a puff of acrid-smelling smoke, the bulb exploded, and the room was plunged into darkness.

'Oh dear,' I thought as I snuggled under the duvet. 'I definitely have a lot of work to do.'

Chapter 6

When I woke up the next day I felt oddly at home. Bright, frosty sunlight streamed through a gap in the thick curtains and I smiled to see that the rain had stopped – for now.

Tugging my fingers through my sleep-tangled hair, I listened for signs of life. Downstairs I could hear the faint sound of Radio Four and murmured voices, so I jumped out of bed, pulled on a jumper and a thick pair of socks – the house was never very warm – and headed towards the noise.

Mum was in the kitchen alone. She was standing, reading *The Guardian* and chewing a slice of toast. I kissed her sleepily and sat down at the table. She plonked a mug of tea and a delicious-smelling muffin in front of me and I frowned. Normally I'd have done a workout at the gym by this time and such an indulgent treat wouldn't have passed my lips. But it smelled so good. Maybe I could just have a taste.

'What are you going to do today?' Mum asked, as I finished my muffin and reached for another.

'Don't you need me to help you at the café?' I said, through a mouthful of crumbs.

Mum shook her head.

'Get yourself settled first,' she said. 'I know you work hard in London – have a couple of days rest before you start toiling for us.'

I smiled at her but I felt uneasy. How long was she expecting me to stay? I hadn't considered being away from work for more than a fortnight. In fact, I'd not taken more than a week off in one go the whole time I'd worked for Lloyd & Lloyd.

'Mum,' I began, then stopped as Suky wandered into the kitchen. She looked thin in her chunky sweater but she had a wide smile on her face and she grabbed me in a tight hug.

'It is so good to see you,' she muttered into my hair.

'You too,' I said as she sat down opposite me and poured herself a cup of tea. I studied her carefully. She'd always been slender, but now her cheekbones stuck out and she had dark circles under her eyes. She'd wrapped a bright pink scarf around her head and, despite her pallor, looked exotic and mysterious like I remembered her as a little girl.

Suky saw me looking at her headscarf and flashed me a rueful smile.

'My hair's already very thin, and I'm worried it's starting to fall out,' she said. 'It's not even the drugs, it's stress. I keep thinking I should cut it short and be done with it.' Her voice wobbled slightly. 'But I'm too scared.'

I reached across the table and took her hand.

'I'll help you,' I said. My voice wobbled too.

Suky gave a shaky laugh. 'Look at us, such a pair of cry-babies,' she said, but her eyes shone with gratitude.

'So,' I said, changing the subject before I got too emotional. 'I found my book last night.'

Mum sat down next to me. 'Did you read it?' she asked.

'Hmm. Sort of,' I said. 'I'm a bit rusty.'

Suky smiled.

'We knew you would be,' she said, taking a bite of toast. 'We don't expect miracles immediately.'

I felt awkward again. How long would they give me before they *did* expect miracles?

'I've been thinking,' I said. 'How about I pick up the slack with all the practical stuff – serving customers, doing the orders,

26

washing the dishes – then Mum, you and Eva can look after the er, magical side of things while Suky gets better. I'll just be there to make up the numbers.' I was embarrassingly hazy about how the whole Three thing worked, but I guessed it would be OK as long as I was actually there, even if I wasn't brilliant at magic.

Suky squeezed my hand again.

'That would be perfect,' she said. Suddenly I felt much happier.

'What's the plan for today, then?' I asked.

'Eva's opening up this morning,' Mum said. 'I'm going to drop Suky in Inverness for her treatment and then take over at the café. Why don't you go for a bit of a walk and have a look round – nothing's changed much – and then meet me at the café later? How does that sound?'

It sounded OK – not as good as a day at work followed by an evening with Dom – but it would do. I grabbed another muffin, just in case I got hungry on the journey, wrapped up warm in the puffa jacket I never wore in London, and headed out into the cold, down the hill towards town.

I'd walked that way a million times before – to school, to the bus stop, to friends' houses, to the pub – and it was comfortingly familiar. I looked at the cottages as I passed, wondering if I still knew anyone who lived there. I doubted it. They'd probably all moved on – as I had.

My phone beeped in my pocket. I fished it out and read the message. It was from Dom.

'Miss U,' it said.

I checked my watch; it was 10am. Dom would almost certainly be in meetings all day, but I decided to break the rules and risk a quick phone call.

'I miss you too,' I said when he answered.

'Yep,' Dom said. He was obviously with someone.

'Can't talk?' I asked with a chuckle.

'That's correct,' he said.

I sniggered. 'Call me later,' I said. 'Sexy.'

Dom coughed. 'I'll follow that up this afternoon,' he said.

Chapter 7

Smiling to myself, I walked into town. Mum was right; not much had changed. Loch Claddach centre was built around an elongated square with the town hall at one end and shops lining each side. There was a Boots and an Oxfam, but besides those, the shops were mostly newsagent's or twee tourist shops selling tartan fridge magnets and stuffed Loch Ness monsters. A few cars were parked in the middle of the square but there was no one around. It was all exactly as I remembered.

Uninspired, I crossed the road. Through the gaps between the buildings on the far side of the square, I could glimpse the inky black water of the loch. The Claddach Café was just a few minutes' walk away, down one of the side streets that led to the waterside, so I decided to pop in and say hello to Eva, have a cup of coffee and watch the world go by.

I walked down towards the loch, shivering in the icy wind that blew across the water. The view was spectacular from here. Despite the cold, the sun was shining brightly and light bounced off the surface of the loch. Beyond it, I could see the purple-green hills and far in the distance, the snowy caps of the mountains. I breathed in deeply. There was so much air and so much space after London. I felt liberated. And, I suddenly realised, very cold.

With numb fingers, I pushed open the door to the café feeling my frozen toes come back to life as the warmth wrapped round me like a blanket. Eva was behind the counter, making a cappuccino for, I assumed, the only other customer who was in the café. That was unusual. Normally the place was packed at this time in the morning – at least it always had been. I shrugged off my coat and wandered over to the counter. Eva was wearing a polka-dot apron splattered with coffee. She had a pair of glasses on the end of her nose, one slung around her neck on a chain and another perched on top of her greying, curly hair.

'Esme,' she said in her soft Yorkshire accent. She came round the counter and opened her arms for a hug.

'Hello, Eva,' I said into her sizeable bosom. She released me, finally, and bustled me over to one of the sofas by the window.

'Lovely Esme, let me look at you,' she said, holding my hands and spreading out my arms. 'Hmm, too thin, too tired, too much hard work,' she frowned. 'A few days up here will see you right.'

I wasn't sure, but I couldn't help smiling. I adored Eva. While Mum and Suky were undoubtedly kind-hearted and generous, they both had a spiky side. Eva – emotionally and physically – was all soft edges.

My Granny had started the café years ago, selling traditional teas and cakes to tourists. There wasn't a whiff of magic about the place, not then. Although she did – obviously – help people with their problems on a personal basis.

When Suky had Harry, she came home for a while, and as Harry grew, Suky's contribution to the café grew too. She began dabbling in tinctures and tonics, selling them to locals for all sorts of ailments. And she persuaded my mum – who'd done a business course in Glasgow and was running from an unhappy love affair – to come home too. So they all rubbed along – Mum, Suky and Gran, and Harry and me. Then, when I was twelve, and high-flying Harry had just started an MBA in the States, Gran died and the magic at home leaked away, just a bit, but enough for Mum and Suky to know they were in trouble. Harry was committed to her studies, and I was too young – they needed to find another witch.

As the last guests departed after Gran's funeral, Mum, Suky, Harry and I sat at the kitchen table feeling a little lost. At least I was. I remember Harry barely lifted her head out of the economics book she was reading. Then there was a knock on the back door and when I opened it, there was Eva.

'Hello,' she said in her matter-of-fact way. 'I think I'm supposed to stay here.'

It sounds crazy, just opening your home up to a stranger. But in the world of witches, it's actually not as weird as it could be. Suky and Mum had sent out a kind of call for help – a celestial SOS – and Eva had answered. So when she arrived on the door-step, they knew exactly why she was there. Basically, Mum and Suky grinned at each other, and that was that. Eva moved into the outbuilding at the bottom of our garden with her husband Allan. They patched it up at first, then slowly made it their home, and even added a studio for Allan, a landscape artist, and a kiln for Eva's ceramics.

Eva said she wasn't sure what made her come to Claddach. She and Allan were in a bad way back then. Their teenage son Simon had been killed in a car accident a couple of years before.

'Existing we were,' Eva once told me. 'Not living.'

Allan had stopped painting, Eva's magic had all but burned out.

'I couldn't see the point,' she said. 'My magic couldn't save Simon and I didn't want anything else.'

And then one morning, the morning of Granny's funeral (though of course she didn't know that at the time), Eva woke up with a new sense of purpose.

'We are needed in Scotland,' she told Allan; sweet, unques-tioning Allan. And they packed their bags and left – driving all day to reach us.

Shortly after they arrived, Allan sold a painting to a card

company – then another and another. Suddenly he was in demand and, for the first time, comfortably off. Eva's ceramics sold well to tourists all over the Highlands and as soon as she met up with Mum and Suky her magic came back in abundance. And so they stayed, and they were happy. And their home became a refuge for teenagers – some placed there officially by social services and some who just found their way there looking for Eva's non-judgemental affection and Allan's calm, steady care.

When I'd left home, angry and upset with Mum and betrayed by Harry, I'd cursed the universe that had led Eva to our garden. If she'd lived further away, she could have been my refuge, I'd thought at the time. But now, I was simply pleased to see her.

Eva smiled at me.

'Is it like you remembered?' she asked.

I nodded, looking through the café's long windows and out over the loch.

'It's like I've never been away,' I said, bewildered by how little had changed in such a long time. 'Do you need a hand?'

Eva looked at the empty café and shook her head.

'It's all under control,' she said with a wry smile.

'In that case, I'll have a latte please.' I was going to make the most of being a customer while I still could.

She punched me gently on the arm.

'Cheeky.' But she got up and began making me a coffee anyway.

I took my drink and a glossy magazine from the rack over to a table, where I sat, ignoring the celebs in my mag and gazing out of the window instead. As I watched a small boat jump across the surface of the loch, the door to the café was flung open and a gust of cold wind rippled the pages of my magazine.

Chapter 8

'Esme! It's true! You are back!'

I looked up. So did Eva. Chloë stood in the doorway, her long red hair lifting in the wind and a frown on her face. I was overjoyed to see her. She'd been my best friend all the way through school. She ignored the other children when they muttered about my odd family and I stuck by her when she was teased for being so tall and gawky. Now she was tall, lean and beautiful with striking auburn hair and creamy white skin – and my family was still odd.

I jumped up to hug her – and close the door behind her because I was freezing.

'I heard you were back,' Chloë said, pulling up a chair. 'Why didn't you call me?'

I grinned at her. The infamous Loch Claddach gossips had clearly been doing a good job.

'I've not even been here a day,' I laughed. 'How did you know I'd arrived?'

Chloë rolled her eyes.

'Mrs Parkinson saw you drive in last night,' she said. 'She called Mum, and Mum called me. I thought you'd be here, so I left the kids with their gran until Rob gets home.'

My smile faltered slightly. In my opinion Rob and the kids were the reason Chloë and I had grown apart. Inseparable at school, we'd remained close when I left Claddach. But after uni, while I threw myself into my work, Chloë married Rob, took a teaching job in Inverness, moved home and squeezed out two children in quick succession. After that we didn't have much in common anymore, though we'd kept in touch with regular emails. I told myself I was bored with Chloë's talk of nappies and nurseries, but the truth was I was a little in awe of her. She seemed like a proper grown up, while I still felt like a child. Now, even though I was pleased to see her, I sat awkwardly opposite her, not sure what to say next.

'So,' I finally began as Eva put a cappuccino in front of Chloë without being asked. 'Is everything still shit?'

Chloë laughed and looked sheepish.

'I was a bit overdramatic in my last email,' she said, sticking her finger in the froth of her coffee. 'It's just things haven't exactly worked out as I planned, you know?'

I nodded, even though in terms of my career, things had worked out exactly as I'd planned.

'I never thought I'd be stuck here, no job and two kids before I'm even thirty.'

'But you're feeling better now?' I asked.

Chloë leaned forward.

'Thanks to Suky,' she said. 'I hadn't told anyone how I was feeling – only you. Not Rob, or my mum. Then I was in here a few weeks ago and Suky brought me a cake I hadn't ordered. You know how she does?'

'I do.' I eyed Chloë's cappuccino, which she hadn't ordered either, suspiciously.

'Anyway, about two days later I bumped into Mary – she's the head at the primary school here – we got chatting and she mentioned they needed someone three days a week to do extra tuition with some of the kids. We had a chat, I taught a lesson for her, blah blah, you know the drill. And now I've got a new job, which is perfect. And then I mentioned that I'd been looking at the MAs in the Open University brochure, Mary made a couple of calls and suddenly the council is funding me to do the course I want. Isn't it funny how these things just happen?'

'Isn't it?' I said drily, glancing at Eva, who was studiously ignoring us.

'I think I was one of the last people Suky helped actually, before . . .' She paused. 'You know.'

I didn't want to talk about Suky's cancer right now. I changed the subject.

'So what's going on here?' I asked, though I didn't really care.

'Ooh well there is some gossip. Have you heard it?'

'I've only just arrived, Chlo,' I said.

She stared at me, as if to say *so?*

'I haven't heard any gossip.'

'There's a hot new man in town,' she said.

'Really?' This was interesting. 'Permanently?' Claddach had a stream of ever-changing arty visitors but no one ever stayed long.

'Apparently so. For the foreseeable anyway. And . . .' She was almost bouncing in her chair with excitement. 'He's American. Some tech millionaire.'

'Probably one of Harry's friends,' I said. Harry's business – a self-help empire – had started online.

Chloë looked deflated.

'Oh do you think?'

'Joke.'

Chloë rolled her eyes and carried on as though I hadn't spoken.

'Anyway, he's hot, rich, American – the women of Claddach are in a frenzy.'

I chuckled.

'Millicent Fry is beside herself,' Chloë said.

'Who's she?'

'Oh she's a treat,' said Chloë. 'One of the rat-race escapees.' Claddach was full of people running from life in Glasgow,

Edinburgh or down south. There were writers, artists, poets, potters, silversmiths – all sorts.

'So what does she do?' I asked.

'She runs the B&B,' Chloë said. 'Only she calls it a boutique hotel.'

She carried on talking, but I had lost interest as self-pity overwhelmed me. All these people escaping the rat race and I couldn't wait to get back to it.

'Mum wants me to stay,' I said, interrupting Chloë's tales of Millicent Fry.

'Will you?'

I shrugged.

'I can't really. There's work . . .' I trailed off, knowing it was a rubbish excuse.

'How are things with your mum?'

'Better. The same. Worse,' I said. 'I don't know. It's going to be strange living in the same house again.'

'Could be just what you need,' Chloë pointed out. 'It's been ten years, Ez, since all the stuff with Jamie . . .'

She gasped and put her hand to her mouth.

'Oh my God, I can't believe I haven't told you!'

'Told me what?' I said. 'What on earth is that?'

A woman was walking past the café wearing a Barbour jacket with a tartan tam o' shanter perched on her blonde curls.

Chloë turned to look at what had caught my eye. She grinned in delight.

'That,' she laughed, 'is Millicent Fry.'

'No!' I said. 'Why is she wearing that hat?'

Chloë chuckled. 'She's not Scottish,' she said. 'But she'd like to be. She wears a lot of tartan.'

Together we watched Millicent walk up the path into the town centre. Then Chloë got up.

'I must go,' she said, giving me a kiss. 'I need to rescue Rob from the children– he's due at work soon. Come round for dinner?'

I agreed to see her later and said goodbye. As Chloë left the café, Mum came in and my good mood left me almost immediately. I knew she was there to do some enchanting and I knew she wanted me to do it too.

'Hello, darling,' she tinkled at me across the empty tables, falsely bright.

I heaved myself up from my comfy seat and slunk across to the counter where Mum and Eva stood.

'Hello,' I said sounding exactly as I had when I was a moody teenager.

'Ready?'

'Not really.' I was nervous, actually. What if I made everything go wrong? My magic wasn't great at the best of times.

'It's all nothing to worry about,' Mum tried her best to reassure me as she and Eva steered me into the kitchen behind the counter, where Eva had started to bake a big bowl of something that smelled yummy.

I forced a smile.

'Just tell me what to do, I'll do it and then I'm out of here,' I said. I didn't mean to be so grumpy but somehow I couldn't help it.

Mum handed me a wooden spoon. 'Stir this.'

I stirred the huge bowl half-heartedly.

'Put some welly into it,' Eva said, as she reached up on to a shelf for a big bag of chopped dates and passed it to me.

'Add these to the mixture,' she said. 'Honestly, don't worry. You're not doing this alone – we're a team here.'

I poured the dates into my mixture and smiled at Eva doubtfully. I wasn't convinced by her breezy good humour.

'You don't know my track record,' I said, thinking of the broken light bulb in my bedroom and the car-hire woman's computer.

'Doesn't matter,' she said again. 'Stop fretting.'

I nodded slowly. 'OK,' I agreed. 'But don't say I didn't warn you.'

Wrinkling my nose, I peered into the bowl I was stirring. It was full of a dark brown, lumpy mixture.

'What is this?' I asked. 'I'm not sure it's supposed to look like this.'

Mum leaned over and looked into the bowl.

'Oh yes it is,' she said. 'It's sticky toffee pudding.'

'And what makes it *special* sticky toffee pudding?' I asked.

Mum and Eva grinned at each other.

'Well, it's not yet,' Mum said. 'But it will be in just a moment. Hold my hand.'

I put down the spoon and took Mum's hand in my slightly sticky fingers. Eva took my other hand and linked with Mum over the bowl. She closed her eyes, so did Mum, but I kept mine open. I wanted to see what was going to happen.

Eva breathed in deeply and began to mutter a stream of strange words. She spoke so quietly her voice was like a breath, yet I could hear everything as clearly as if she were speaking straight into my ear.

As she spoke, time in the kitchen seemed to stand still. Everything was completely silent – I couldn't even hear the noise of the coffee machine in the café or the waves crashing on the shore anymore. Then, slowly, over the bowl, the air began to sparkle as though someone had shaken a pot of glitter high above the kitchen. I gasped as the sparkles floated downwards into the sticky toffee pudding and disappeared.

Mum dropped my hand.

'That's it,' she said briskly.

'That's it?' I asked, still peering into the bowl. 'What have you – we – just done exactly?'

'It's for keeping secrets,' Mum said.

I raised an eyebrow in disbelief.

Mum flicked me with a tea towel.

'Look as sceptical as you like,' she said. 'It works.'

'And who's it for?' I asked.

'Mrs Unwin.'

'What secrets does she have? Actually, don't tell me. It's probably better if I don't know.'

This was exactly why I had a problem with what Mum and the others got up to in the tearoom. Unlike our ancestors from hundreds of years ago, and even my Gran just a few years ago, they didn't always wait for people to come to them for help.

'We can't go around shouting about what we are, Esme. These are suspicious times,' Mum always said when I challenged her. 'But we do have to be proactive. It is the 21st century after all.'

Being proactive, according to Mum, Eva and Suky, meant being the eyes and ears of the village. They watched people meet for coffee, listened to conversations and paid attention to what wasn't said. Then they interfered.

'We help,' said Mum. I wasn't so sure.

Say, for example, Mum happened to overhear Old Mrs Lewis telling Mrs Parkinson that she'd seen her granddaughter kissing a boy who was definitely not her boyfriend. She'd serve them both up a portion of this dark, moistly sweet, sticky toffee pudding – whether they'd asked for it or not – and somehow the girl's stolen kisses would stay a secret.

Or, if Eva chatted to Chloë about how difficult she was finding being a mum, Chloë would find a piece of millionaire's shortbread in front of her, warm and chocolatey and oozing with soft toffee. And by the time she'd eaten it, she'd be appreciating her riches.

'I've got the two best kids in the world,' she'd say and head off, misty-eyed, back to her family.

They'd even come up with a recipe for coffee cake – known among themselves as spill the beans cake – that made whoever ate it open their heart and let out whatever was on their mind.

I thought it was wrong to dispense unwanted advice and interfere in people's private lives in this way. I'd been on the receiving end of Mum's meddling myself with disastrous conse-quences which made my feelings on the matter even stronger and ironically made Mum and Suky even less likely to listen to my objections – because they thought I was too emotional about it all. But whatever my opinion, I couldn't deny that the café was enormously successful. At least it always had been. It was strangely quiet today. And, even though our customers weren't always aware of the helping hand they'd been given, they did flock to see Mum, Eva and Suky whenever they felt they needed to share a problem, get an energy boost or even share good news.

Thoughtfully I licked sticky toffee pudding mixture from the spoon.

'Don't eat that!' Mum cried. I laughed.

'I don't have any secrets I need to keep,' I lied, thinking of Dom and how much trouble it would cause if everyone – Mum, Chloë, people at work . . . Rebecca – found out about our relationship.

Mum took the spoon from me and put it in the dishwasher.

'I was thinking about the health inspector,' she said. 'If he saw you doing that, he'd close us down.'

Chapter 9

Relieved it was all over, and with no ill effects as far as I could see, I decided to leave Mum and Eva to it and go out for some fresh air. I bundled myself up in my thick coat and decided to go for a walk round the loch.

Wrapping my scarf round my neck, I tramped across the stony beach to the water's edge and looked across to the other side. Claddach was a small loch, a puddle really, compared to some, so I could see the far end clearly. It was said to be as deep as it was long, however, and I believed it. The water was still and peaty black at the centre. At the edge, where I stood, small waves lapped at the shingle and further out, the water was being whipped into small peaks by the wind. The mountains were purple against the bright blue frosty sky as they loomed over the loch. It was bleak but it was beautiful.

I picked up a flat stone and skidded it across the waves. It jumped once . . . twice . . . three times then sank into the murky water. Rubbish. I'd lost my touch. I tried again . . . four . . . five . . . better.

Behind me, the shingle crunched and suddenly another stone flew past my arm. I watched as it skipped five, six times.

'Yes!' said a voice and I turned to see who had gatecrashed my game.

It was a man. A rather handsome man, actually. He was wearing running gear and because he was higher up the steeply shelving beach than I was, my eyes were level with his toned, tanned thighs. Thighs that told me this wasn't a local man – this must be Chloë's hot American.

'Sorry,' he smiled and his eyes crinkled up at the corners in a way that made him look like a preppy George Clooney. 'I can't resist a bit of competition.'

'You won,' I pointed out, still annoyed at his interruption.

'I always do,' he said. I didn't doubt it. He looked like he'd spent his life winning.

The American stuck out his hand for me to shake.

'Brent Portland,' he said.

I shook his hand.

'Esme McLeod.'

'Going this way?' he nodded in the direction of Mum's house. I thought of a reason to go the other way – I was no fan of small talk at the best of times – but came up with nothing.

'I am,' I said. We began walking back up the beach to the road. Brent was nice looking, I couldn't deny, though he wasn't my type. He was an all-American, clean-cut guy with tousled dark hair, good skin and startlingly white even teeth.

He was fairly short for a man – about 5'9 or 10' – but he still towered over me.

'So Esme McLeod,' he said as we walked. 'I've been in town for about two weeks now. How come today is the first time we've met?'

'I just got here myself,' I said.

'So you're a stranger here too?' He gave me an eager grin. 'How are you finding it?'

'I'm not exactly a stranger,' I said. 'I grew up here. My mum runs the café – back there.' I pointed back the way we'd come.

Brent's eyes widened.

'I love that place,' he said. 'It's so cute. And the cakes – wow!' He patted his very flat stomach. 'I need to stay away from those.'

41

His over-enthusiastic response to everything was beginning to grate on me, so I was pleased to see the path I needed to take.

'I have to go,' I said. 'Enjoy your run.'

Brent was already bouncing on the spot, ready to jog off. He made me feel weary just looking at him.

'Nice to meet you Esme McLeod,' he said over his shoulder as he took off at a cracking pace. 'See you around.'

Chapter 10

'Bye Mum!' I yelled as I shut the front door later that evening 'Don't wait up!'

Tucking a bottle of wine under my arm, I headed down the hill to Chloë's house for dinner. Chloë had ended up living close to where she grew up, round the corner from her parents on the new estate, so the walk to her house felt like old times. It was freezing and the wind flapped my jeans against my legs and blew the rain into my face. I walked along hunched against the weather, looking forward to seeing Chloë again, but nervous about seeing her at home with her husband Rob, their little boy, Olly, and their baby, Matilda. Her home life was very different from my solo evenings in my flat with a bottle of wine and a Netflix binge.

I turned into the new estate where Chloë lived. Her house was on the corner. A small trike lay on its side in the front garden and a muddy Land Rover stood in the drive. It all looked very grown up.

Suddenly nervous, I rang the doorbell. Footsteps thundered down the hallway towards me and I took a step backwards in alarm. Chloë opened the door, a cross, red-faced baby on her hip and a small boy with a wonky fringe and huge, curious brown eyes peeking out at me from behind her knees.

'A picture of domestic bliss,' I said, kissing Chloë on the cheek.

'Not quite,' she said wryly. 'Olly, this is Esme. Say hello.'

I bent down and shook Olly's tiny, slightly damp hand. He regarded me with mild interest.

'I did a standing-up wee,' he said solemnly.

'How lovely,' I said, standing up again and wiping my hand on my trousers. I was never sure what to say to small children. Olly raced off as Chloë pulled the wine out of my arms and beckoned to the kitchen.

'Come on Mary Poppins,' she said. 'Let's crack this open.'

I followed her down the hall, its walls covered in photos of the children, and into the kitchen. One end had been extended into a conservatory and the rain pounded noisily on the glass roof. Inside though it was warm and cosy. On the fridge were several of Olly's drawings and a chart with gold stars on, and something that smelled delicious was bubbling on the hob. It all felt very homely and with a sudden burst of affection I hugged Chloë. She plopped Matilda on to the floor, where she began to wail in self-pity, and hugged me back.

'This is gorgeous,' I said over Matilda's roars. 'The house, the kids, everything.'

'I know,' she said. 'I am lucky. Sometimes it's hard to remember. But I'm so excited about my new job – it's just perfect.'

She looked at me slyly.

'Wasn't it so weird that it just happened like that,' she said, opening a drawer in search of a corkscrew. 'One minute I'm chatting to Suky, the next I'm in the running for the perfect job.'

I took the bottle from her and found the corkscrew. 'Very weird,' I said without looking at her.

I poured us both large glasses of wine, stuck what was left of the bottle in the door of the fridge and gave Matilda the cork to play with. She put it into her mouth and sucked happily.

'So, anyway, how's Rob's job going?'

Chloë scowled. 'Don't change the subject,' she said, taking the cork away from Matilda, who howled in rage, and giving her a battered rag doll instead. 'I saw Harry last week, but she was too busy to chat.'

I rolled my eyes. Harry was always too busy.

Chloë ignored me.

'So if Harry's gone again, does that mean you've come back to, you know, *help* at the café?'

Chloë was about the only person who knew the truth about my family. We'd been friends for a few years when she stumbled upon my secret. We were fourteen and I was just starting to reject witchcraft – I wanted to be like the girls from school, gossiping about make-up and boys, but instead I felt like I was on the outside of their gang, looking in. Chloë understood how I felt – with her gawky frame and carrot-top hair, she was also a bit of an outsider. We stuck together and I loved having a best friend to hang out with, but I still hated being a witch and avoided using magic whenever possible.

One day, Mum and I were having one of our regular shouting matches. She'd asked me to help out at the café, and I'd refused, telling her I didn't want to do magic ever again. Like I did every time she asked. I was frustrated at her refusal to understand my feelings and she was hurt by my rejection. It was an explosive combination and tensions were running high.

'What do you want from me?' I'd yelled.

'I want you to love yourself,' Mum had replied quietly. 'I want you to accept who you are.'

I was furious.

'Like this?' I whirled round and sent a shower of pink sparks shooting from my fingers to the kitchen radio. It started blaring French pop and Mum winced.

'Or what about this?' I sent another sparkly shower to the light switch and the kitchen lights flashed off and on.

Mum tried to speak, but I wouldn't let her. I shot sparks across the kitchen again and again, turning on appliances, switching off

45

lights and opening and shutting cupboard doors. Then, just as I was about to run out of energy, I spun round and saw Chloë standing open-mouthed at the back door. As I paused, horrified at what she'd seen, Mum did her thing and restored order to the kitchen. Then, without saying a word, she got up from the table and left Chloë and me alone.

I couldn't speak; I was so scared that I'd cry. Chloë was my best friend and I'd probably lost her forever. We stared at each other for a moment, then Chloë came over to me and looped her arm through mine.

'Always thought you were a bit peculiar,' she'd said cheerfully. 'Shall we go ice skating at the weekend?'

And that was that. No shock, or disbelief. Just a mild, genuine interest and lots of love and support. In fact, Chloë was far more accepting of me, than I was of myself.

Now I looked at her slightly shamefully.

'I said I'd do a bit,' I admitted. 'I'm pretty rusty. I only ever use it to find a parking space or if I've made a mess in the kitchen.'

Chloë grinned.

'You never know Ez,' she said. 'You might just discover that you like it.'

46

Chapter 11

Much later, we sat on Chloë's sofa and chinked our glasses together. The children were asleep, finally, looking like little angels in their beds upstairs, and Chloë's husband Rob was opening a tub of Häagen-Dazs in the kitchen. I was full, slightly tipsy and for the first time since I'd met Harry in London, I actually felt quite content.

'Welcome home,' Chloë said.

I beamed at her. 'It's strange to be back,' I said honestly. 'I'm in bits about Suky's illness and it was horrible to have come back so suddenly.' I took a slurp of my wine. 'But it's actually a relief to have some distance from work and stuff.'

Rob came into the living room balancing three bowls of ice cream precariously. He handed one each to Chloë and me, then sat down on the chair next to us. I looked at him suspiciously. I'd liked Rob immediately. He was a big, blond man with the broad build and crooked nose of a rugby player. Over dinner he'd made me laugh with stories about his work as a police officer in Inverness and I'd warmed to him as I watched him play with the children. Most importantly for me, I could see he adored Chloë. He definitely had my approval but even so, I hadn't expected him to be part of our girly catch-up.

'What stuff?' Chloë asked me, digging into her ice cream. 'What do you need distance from? Is it a man? You never mention men in your emails.'

I glanced at Rob. He seemed as eager as Chloë to hear my news and didn't appear to have any plans to leave. I licked the sweet ice cream off the back of my spoon –it was literally years since I'd eaten anything so indulgent – and smiled ruefully at Chloë.

'I do have a sort-of boyfriend,' I admitted. 'He's called Dom.'

Chloë squealed. 'I knew you were being cagey about something,' she said joyfully. 'So come on, what's he like? Where did you meet him?'

I shifted on the sofa, suddenly feeling uncomfortable.

'I met him at work,' I began. 'He's gorgeous. Tall, well-dressed, really handsome.' I smiled to myself as I thought of Dom, slick in his grey suit, winking sneakily at me in a meeting. Then I thought of him rushing home to meet Rebecca and frowned.

'He sounds fab,' Chloë said eagerly. 'Will he be coming up?'

'Erm,' I said. 'It's difficult . . .'

I trailed off. Rob sat forward in his chair.

'He's married isn't he?'

I gasped. 'How do you know?'

Rob grinned. 'I've interviewed loads of suspects,' he said, relaxing back into the cushions. 'You're rubbish at covering things up.'

I bristled. 'I am not covering anything up,' I said haughtily. 'And I am not a suspect.' I drained my wine and held my empty glass out for Chloë to refill.

She glugged the remains of the bottle into my glass and scowled at me.

'How could you, Esme?' she said. 'His poor wife. Have you met her?'

'Never. I don't really know anything about her. They're getting divorced, Dom says. He says they got married too young. He says . . .'

'She doesn't understand him,' Chloë and Rob chorused.

Embarrassed, I averted my eyes from Chloë's disappointed expression and studied my feet instead. I felt ashamed. Unbelievable as it sounded, I'd never really considered Rebecca's side of things before. I'd always seen myself as the victim – the person unlucky enough to have fallen for a married man. Suddenly I realised it was Rebecca who was the unlucky one to be married to a man who was cheating.

Chloë put her hand on my arm.

'Is he really going to leave his wife?' she asked gently.

I shook my head. Suddenly I felt close to tears although I couldn't understand why.

'I don't think so,' I said. 'He says he loves me, but nothing changes.' I sniffed loudly. 'I don't want them to actually. I'm happy with things as they are.'

'I don't believe you,' Rob said. I was definitely starting to dislike him.

'Rob, be nice.' Chloë warned.

I smiled at her gratefully.

'I don't want Dom to leave Rebecca,' I said firmly.

'Are you trying to convince us or yourself?' Chloë asked. I winced and shrank back into the sofa cushions under her glare.

'Do you love him?' asked Rob.

I looked at him, startled.

'Do you?' Chloë repeated.

I looked into my glass and swirled the wine up its edges.

'I don't know,' I said quietly. 'I just don't know.'

I felt unsettled as I walked back up the hill from Chloë's. Talking about Dom was so unusual – I'd kept him secret from my few friends in London and never mentioned him to Mum – that it had felt odd to discuss our relationship. Plus, Chloë and Rob had asked me the questions I knew I should really have asked myself. Did I want Dom to leave Rebecca? Did I love him? I wasn't sure, I realised as I quietly let myself into the sleeping house and crept up the stairs to my room. And if I wasn't sure, what did that mean? Did our relationship have no future? Did I really want to spend the rest of my life sharing the man I (possibly) loved?

Longing for reassurance, I pulled out my phone and sent Dom a text.

'Night darling,' I typed. 'Call when U can.'

Straightaway my phone bleeped in reply.

'Love U,' Dom sent.

Overjoyed and feeling much better about things, I walked over to the window to shut the curtains. Down below me, on the street, a dark shadow caught my eye. I paused and strained my eyes through the night to see what it was.

'Strange,' I said thoughtfully. It was a man, standing still. He seemed to be staring at our house though it was hard to tell exactly in the moonlight. I couldn't decide what to do. In London I'd have grabbed my phone and called the police, but things were different here. Maybe it was just a tourist who'd got lost, so I didn't want to be too hasty. I watched from behind the curtain as the man turned and began to walk back down the hill. As he passed under a streetlamp he moved his head to look back at our house and I gasped in surprise. It was Brent Portland – the man I'd met on the beach earlier. What was he doing up here so late? There wasn't much to see up here – it wasn't a great location for a midnight stroll.

Feeling uneasy, I let the curtain drop and snuggled into bed wondering if there was more to Brent than a nice smile.

Chapter 12

'What happens if you're late?' I asked Suky, turning the ignition key again.

'They're not going to turn me away,' she said. 'It's radiotherapy – you don't need a ticket.'

She was bundled up in the passenger seat wearing a duffle coat like Paddington Bear's and an enormous furry hat. I turned the key again. This time the battered 2CV Mum and Suky shared made a small noise like a cough and stopped again. There was an expectant pause. Suky looked at me.

'Go on then,' she said. 'I can't help I'm afraid – even a tiny bit of magic wipes me out at the moment.'

'Oh,' I said. 'You want me to start the car? With magic?'

Suky looked at me as though I were simple.

'Yes please,' she said.

I took a deep breath.

'OK,' I said to myself. 'Start the car with magic. How hard can it be?'

I waggled my fingers in the direction I thought the engine should be in. Nothing happened. I did it again. This time there was a pop, and a small column of smoke spiralled up from beneath the bonnet. Suky raised her eyebrows at me from beneath her furry hat. Embarrassed, I opened my door and got out of the car.

'I'll, erm, just go and sort it out,' I said. I opened the bonnet – after a couple of attempts – wafted away smoke and peered inside. I couldn't decide if it was riskier to try and mend it with magic or without.

'Can I give you ladies a hand?' I jumped in surprise and banged my head. Brent had pulled up alongside me in a Range Rover. He was leaning out of the driver's window with a cheery smile.

'We're having a bit of car trouble,' Suky said. 'Unfortunate timing as I've got a hospital appointment to get to.'

'Suky,' I said crossly. I hated people knowing what I considered to be our business.

'Esme had a hire car until yesterday but it's gone back now,' she carried on. I sighed. Once Suky started sharing there was no stopping her. I just hoped she didn't mention that I'd not returned the car to the airport – instead I'd come downstairs yesterday morning and found the car gone and the paperwork neatly stacked at the front door. Mum had *sorted it out* for me.

'I'm no mechanic,' Brent said. 'But I am at a loose end. How about I give you guys a lift?'

I opened my mouth to say he was very kind, but really we could manage without his help, but Suky was already climbing out of our car and into the passenger seat of the Range Rover.

I let the bonnet close with a crash, and climbed in too. It was an enormous car with shiny leather seats. Maybe the rumours were true and Brent really was a millionaire.

I didn't have long to wait to find out. As we headed towards Inverness, Suky quizzed our driver about what he was doing in Claddach.

'I just needed a break, I guess,' he told her. 'My mom's family were all from Scotland and I wanted to come see it.'

'Do you like it?' Suky asked.

'I love it.' From the back seat, I sighed. Of course he loved it. He loved everything. 'It's nothing like I'd expected, but I love it.

I'm actually thinking about getting a place here so I can come back whenever I want.'

'Goodness,' said Suky. 'Your work must be flexible?'

I smiled to myself. Good old Suky, fishing for information.

'I work for myself,' Brent said. 'Which way from here?'

Suky directed him towards the hospital, but wouldn't be put off from finding out more.

'What line of work are you in?'

Brent smiled at her. 'A bit of this, bit of that,' he said. 'I did have my own company but I sold it and that gave me the freedom to pursue some other interests.'

'It's the next entrance,' Suky said. Brent pulled the car into the hospital grounds. 'What other interests?'

Brent drove neatly into a parking space and turned off the engine before he answered.

'Politics, mainly,' he said. 'I act as a consultant on some aspects of policy.'

Despite myself I was impressed. My knowledge of American politics came, I had to admit, mostly from one seminar at university and *The West Wing*, but I found it fascinating. I resolved to talk to Brent about his job another time.

I jumped down from the Range Rover's high back door and helped Suky out. Then I turned to face Brent.

'Thank you,' I said.

'No problem.' He kissed Suky on the cheek and she flushed like a schoolgirl. 'Good luck with everything. What time shall I come get you?'

'Oh we can get a taxi,' I said. But Brent wouldn't hear of it.

'It's no trouble,' he said. 'I'm going to wander round Inverness and I'll get you later. Give me your phone.'

Meekly, I handed it over. He rang his phone from mine, then cancelled the call.

'Now you have my number,' he said. 'Call me when you're through.'

He got back into his car and turned the key.

'See you later,' he called through the window. And he drove away.

Suky linked her arm through mine.

'He's a nice chap,' she said as we walked into the hospital.

'He seems to be,' I said, still not convinced.

'Oh Esme, you never like anyone at first,' Suky said with a smile. She was right. I was naturally very suspicious of everyone's motives and didn't trust anyone when I first met them. 'You should lighten up a bit.'

I didn't feel very much like lightening up as we walked into the oncology unit. It seemed so wrong that Suky was going there.

Suky had gone quiet too, gazing out of the window at the gloomy views of dreich Inverness. I took her hand, squeezing it gently. She squeezed back.

'Who's your man, then?' she said.

Surprised, I let go of her hand.

'Which man?' I said casually. I hadn't told any of my family about Dom – I knew they'd disapprove when they found out he was married and, to be quite honest, I was a little bit ashamed of myself already.

Suky laughed.

'The man you text all the time,' she said. 'The one who makes your face light up when he calls.'

I'd been rumbled. Blushing, I tried to change the subject, but Suky wouldn't give up.

'Come on, Esme,' she wheedled. 'Tell your old auntie some gossip!'

'Oh look!' I sang, as a nurse came towards us. 'They're expecting you!'

Suky gave me a sharp look.

'I'm not giving up,' she said, greeting the nurse. I ignored her.

Once Suky had been seen by the consultant and was ready to go in for her treatment, we had some time to wait. I went down to the shop to grab a coffee and when I came back Suky was asleep, so I settled down next to her and scrolled through my phone.

'Oh no you don't,' Suky said loudly, opening her eyes and snatching the phone from my hand. 'Tell me what's going on.'

I grabbed it back.

'Nothing is going on,' I growled at her.

She gave me a winning smile.

'I have very little pleasure in my life,' she said with a wink. 'All I ask is that my favourite niece shares her news with me . . .'

I didn't point out that I was her only niece. Instead, with an exaggerated sigh I gave in. It was actually a relief to talk to someone after days – weeks – months – of keeping my relationship with Dom under wraps.

'He's called Dom,' I began. 'We've been seeing each other for a while – quite a long while in fact.' I paused.

'So why do you look so miserable?'

I looked down at my phone and rubbed away an invisible smudge on the screen.

'Is it not going well?'

Suddenly I felt close to tears. I looked up from my Instagram feed.

'He's married,' I whispered.

Suky covered my hand with hers. I looked at her thin fingers and the veins showing through her pale, papery skin, and I felt ashamed. My problems were meaningless compared with hers. I squeezed her fingers gently but I couldn't bring myself to meet her eyes.

'Do you love him?" Suky asked gently.

I played with the chunky silver ring Suky wore on her middle finger, it was too loose now and it spun round easily. Did I love Dom? That seemed to be all I was asking myself at the moment.

I shrugged.

'That's the problem,' I said. 'I don't know.'

'Well, that's what you need to find out.'

I nodded slowly. Suky was right. It seemed my relationship with Dom was at a crossroads and being away from him had brought everything to a head. I knew I had to decide if I wanted to be with him forever – and if he wanted that too, then we couldn't keep going as we were, he'd have to tell Rebecca the truth – or if I wanted to call everything off and strike out on my own.

Suddenly I felt desperate to change the subject.

'So when is Harry coming back?' I asked brightly.

Suky looked at me closely, but she realised I was done talking about Dom and let it go.

'She should be back any day,' she said. 'I'm worried about her but she won't talk to me.'

I had to admit that was odd. Suky and Harry were as close as they could be; more like sisters than mother and daughter. Suky had been young when Harry was born, and she'd brought her up on her own. No one really knew much about Harry's dad – I didn't even know his name, and I didn't know if Harry did. Suky met him back in the 70s when she was following the hippy trail in India. She never talked much about what she got up to over there, but apparently she came back to Scotland glowing and growing, and gorgeous, olive-skinned, dark-haired Harmony was born a few months later.

It was such a shame that after having grown up such close mates, Harry now made me feel on edge, like I was waiting for something bad to happen. And sometimes, not always, but sometimes, it did.

So I had to admit I was pleased she wasn't around at the moment. But Suky was obviously missing her and I knew I'd be off the hook when it came to magic if Harry was here.

Suky gazed out of the window of the ward.

'Harry thinks I could do with a bit of help,' she said.

'What kind of help?'

'Ooh you know. Our kind of help.' Suky didn't look at me.

I frowned.

'I thought we couldn't meddle in medical stuff,' I said, confused.

'Well, no. Not usually.' Suky looked proud. 'But Harry's been doing some research and she says she's found something that could work.'

I was dubious.

'Have you spoken to Mum and Eva about this?'

Suky shook her head.

'Talk to them before you do anything,' I begged. Magic was out of my comfort zone at the best of times. Changing the rules was way too much for me to take in.

'I'm not going to do anything,' she said. She looked very sad for a moment. 'My magic isn't really working just now.'

I had realised her power was dimmed, so I nodded.

'It'll come back though, right?' I said. 'Eva's came back.'

'Hopefully,' Suky said. She rested her head against the pillow on her chair. 'Once all this is over. But . . .'

'What?' I asked. Suky was always so confident, it shook me up to see her so unsure of herself.

'Before I found out about the cancer, I knew something was up,' she said. 'Some of my spells were going wrong.'

'Wrong?'

'Not working. Sometimes working too well.'

'Harry said there had been a bit of trouble at the café,' I suddenly remembered. 'Is that what she meant?'

Suky nodded.

'What sort of thing?'

'Stuff I did myself,' she said. 'Not the other bits that Eva and your mum do. Just the things people actually asked me for help with.'

I grimaced. Somehow the fact that it was help that people had sought that had gone wrong seemed worse.

'The first one was that prickly woman from the newsagent,' she said.

'Was she prickly before her spell went wrong?'

Suky made a face.

'Yes,' she said. 'And worse after. She wanted a happy holiday. She said she and her husband had been saving up for this trip to see their son in Australia and they wanted it to be the holiday of a lifetime.'

'And was it?'

'Well, yes.' Suky screwed her whole face up. 'Not in the way she meant, though. More in the emergency landings, lost travellers' cheques, cancelled hotel bookings and, erm, snake bite, way.'

I stared at her.

'Yowzers,' I said. 'That's not good.'

'Another one came to ask me for good luck for her daughter who had a job interview . . .'

'And?'

Suky gave a small cough.

'Well, let's just say she didn't get the job.'

Despite myself I giggled.

'It doesn't sound too bad,' I said. 'What about the spells that worked too well?'

'One woman wanted to add a bit of spice to her marriage,' Suky said, lowering her voice. 'I think she'd been reading *Fifty Shades of Grey*.'

'Oh no.'

Suky nodded, grim-faced.

'She was insatiable,' she whispered. 'Dragging him down alleyways, even. I'm not sure he minded, but when the spell wore off poor Millicent must have been mortified.'

'Millicent?' I said, thinking of the woman with the tam o' shanter.

'Yes, she's the reason I'm so worried,' Suky went on. 'Have you noticed anything about the café?'

'It's not very busy,' I said, trying to be diplomatic.

She winced.

'That's what I'm afraid of. You know what Claddach is like

– everyone knows everyone else. Well, some of the spells that went wrong were for people who like to talk – especially that Millicent and the prickly one from the newsagent. There's nothing they like more than a good gossip.'

'And you're worried they're telling people their spells didn't work?'

'Well, worse than that, really,' she said. 'I'm more worried they're talking about us – and turning folk against us.'

She paused.

'In my experience,' she said. 'People are accepting of witches as long as we're doing what they want us to do. If things go wrong, they turn very quickly.'

Suky looked so worried that I wanted to reassure her, even though I'd seen how quiet the café was. I was fairly sure worrying over work wasn't the best way to spend the time while you were waiting for your radiotherapy session.

'I'm sure it's nothing,' I lied. 'It's probably just a blip and a few unfortunate coincidences. I think perhaps all the worry over your illness is making you a bit paranoid.'

'Maybe you're right,' Suky said. She looked slightly happier.

We spent the rest of her time in the hospital chatting about anything and everything trivial and inane. Celebrities' haircuts. The latest drama in *EastEnders*. Whether that reality star was pregnant again. But I kept thinking about what Suky had said about the customers at the café. Could she be right about people turning against them?

When the session was over, I called Brent.

'I'm just around the corner,' he told me. 'Be there in five.'

Suky was wiped out and wanted to sit in the back, so I was forced to climb into the passenger seat for the trip home. Dreading making small talk, I tried to study the landscape, but Brent was determined to make me chat.

And actually, once I'd lost my sulkiness, I discovered he was really interesting.

'I just got out at the right time,' he told me about his property business, which he'd sold just before the last recession. 'And then a friend, who'd gone into politics, recommended me for a role. I worked on an election campaign and then when it was all over, I decided to take a break for a while.'

He wasn't married, he told me, and had broken up with his fiancée during the campaign.

'Working twenty-hour days doesn't really make for a happy family life,' he said with a wry smile.

By the time we got home, I'd almost started to warm to this preppy American with his overenthusiastic approach to life.

As we pulled up outside Mum's house, he turned to me.

'Suky has to have radiotherapy every day, right?' he said.

I nodded. 'For three weeks.'

'Let me drive her,' he said.

I shook my head. 'No, it's too much.'

'Nonsense. It's not a long drive and it's better for her to go in comfort.'

I could see he was right.

'If you're sure,' I said.

'Positive.' He beamed at me, his teeth dazzling white in the gloomy light.

'You see,' Suky said, as I helped her into the house. 'I told you he was nice.'

Chapter 13

But Suky's next treatment was delayed when she came down with a cold. I was woken by voices the next morning, then the front door banged. I gave in and swung my legs out of bed and stomped, bleary-eyed, into the kitchen to pour myself a coffee.

There was no sign of Mum or Suky but Eva was there, looking disgustingly perky in a pink tunic covered in tiny mirrors and reading *The Guardian*.

'Morning,' I said, sitting opposite her. 'Where's everyone gone?'

'Suky's come down with a terrible cold,' Eva said. 'We're not sure if she can still go to the hospital, so she and Tess have gone to see the doctor. He's been great through all this – he'll tell her what to do.'

I was impressed.

'Doctor's appointment on a Saturday, eh?' I smiled. 'That'd never happen in London.'

'Well, it's mostly because we know James,' Eva pointed out. 'His dad has been a good friend to all of us.'

With my head bent over my coffee, I froze.

'James Brodie?' I repeated. 'My James?'

Eva laughed, then stopped when she saw my face.

'Oh sweetheart, did no one tell you? Yes, your James. He's come home to take over his dad's practice for a while.' She got up and dropped a kiss on the top of my head. 'You're not upset are you?'

'It was a long time ago,' I said in a squeaky voice. 'I'm over it now.'

'Good,' Eva said, watching me carefully.

I forced myself to smile at her in an over-it kind of way.

'What are you doing today?' I asked, trying hard to keep my voice less squeaky.

'No rest for the wicked,' she said happily. 'I'm off for a walk round the loch, then I'm going to open up. Fancy coming?'

I shook my head.

'I'll come down later,' I said. I really wanted to be alone and absorb the news that Jamie was back in town. Jamie. My first true love and the reason I'd left all those years ago.

Eva scooped up her purse and keys from underneath our fat black cat, Bonnie, who looked most put out at being woken up. I knew how she felt. She jumped down from the chair and stalked snootily out of the cat flap while Eva walked, far less snootily, out of the front door.

I sat at the kitchen table with my head in my hands. James Brodie. My emotions were all over the place as it was, without this blast from the past coming back into my life. I'd known Jamie had wanted to be a doctor like his GP dad, but the last I heard he was off working in disaster zones for the Red Cross or something. Never in a million years had I expected him to be in Claddach too. I couldn't believe Chloë hadn't mentioned it. Or had she? I vaguely remembered her gasping when he'd come up in conversation . . . oh but then I'd been sidetracked by the woman in the tam o' shanter and we'd not gone back to Jamie.

I'd met Jamie when I was fifteen. As a teenager I knew getting good exam results was my ticket out of Loch Claddach and so I'd thrown myself into my studies, poring over my books for hours after school and at weekends.

Mum made me go out for a walk every day, practically forcing me into a jacket and pushing me down the hill.

'A healthy mind in a healthy body,' she'd cry, waving me off as I trudged down the road. But soon I grew to like my walks. Back then I was desperately embarrassed by my strange family and the hustle and bustle of life at home and in the café was almost too much for my self-conscious, painfully shy teenage self to bear. I rejected my magic and rudely avoided Mum's attempts to get me interested in the family business. I longed to get away and the silence of the loch gave me a much-needed escape.

One wintery day, after a huge storm had raged across the loch for most of the night, I was walking along my usual route along the shore when I came across a massive boulder that had been dislodged from the foot of the cliffs by the wind and rain. Where it had been was now a small cave, hidden from the road by the cliffs and sheltered from the gale whipping across the water by the boulder itself. Eagerly I scrambled across the shingle and ducked into the cave. It was small, I could touch the walls with my arms outspread, but it was dry and – bliss – so quiet. I loved it.

I'd gone home that day and got a blanket and some candles as well as a pile of books and my Walkman. Then, every time I'd wanted peace and quiet, I'd headed to my rocky refuge and lost myself in a novel.

As winter loosened its grip and the daffodils bloomed, my exams approached and I arrived at my cave one day to find someone else there. It was a tall, gangly boy about my own age. He was wearing a dark blue Scotland rugby shirt and sitting against the stony wall, his long legs bent up awkwardly. He had floppy dark brown hair that curled over his collar – 'wasted on a boy', my Gran would've said – and he was reading my copy of *Pride and Prejudice*.

Hearing me approach, he looked up and grinned.

'I think Lizzie is a bit of a drip,' he said. 'No wonder Darcy is so snotty with her.'

Outraged, I darted forward and pulled the book from his hands. 'She is not a drip,' I said. 'And who are you?'

'It was better on the telly than in the book,' the boy said, getting to his feet and holding out his hand. 'James Brodie.'

'It was good on the telly,' I admitted. I had watched the BBC adaptation with handsome Colin Firth as brooding Mr Darcy over and over again. I shook the boy's hand cautiously.

'Esme McLeod,' I scowled. 'This is my place.'

'I love what you've done with it,' Jamie said cheekily. He screwed up his nose. 'Can I share it?'

I opened my mouth to say no. My cave was my sanctuary and I didn't want anyone else there. But instead, for reasons that I never really understood, I said yes. And pretty much every time I went to the cave after that, Jamie was there too.

Thinking of Jamie was giving me a headache now so I stood up and poured myself another cup of coffee to take upstairs with me. I thought I might feel better – more in control – if I had a shower and got dressed.

As I shampooed my hair and let the warm water wash away my aches, I thought back to that first spring with Jamie.

He had been a pupil at the nearby posh boys' school, which was why I'd not met him before. His dad had recently taken over the GP's surgery in Loch Claddach and the family had moved to the village from Inverness.

Jamie was studying for his exams too, so we'd often test each other on French vocab or quotes from *To Kill a Mockingbird*. He'd patiently explain chemistry over and over to me, while I (rather less patiently) would take him through the causes of the Second World War.

'So is he your boyfriend then?' Chloë asked one afternoon as we waited for the bus after our English exam.

'No.' I kicked at a tuft of grass. 'He's just a pal.'

'But you do fancy him?' Chloë teased.

I looked down the road to see if the bus was on its way.

'He's nice,' I muttered. 'He makes me laugh.'

Neither Chloë nor I had much luck with boys. Before she grew into her looks, she was tall and gawky with skinny limbs and red hair that made her stand out in any crowd. I was small and blonde – not glam blonde like Carole Murphy in our class who was fifteen and looked twenty-five – but transparently fair with a blue tinge to my skin and a boyish figure. We talked endlessly about kissing and who fancied who, but while our classmates were tormenting themselves about whether it was the right time for them to sleep with their latest flame, neither of us had ever even had a boyfriend.

Now the vague hope that Jamie might fancy me crossed my mind. He was certainly attentive and he sought my company almost every day. I blushed at the thought and changed the subject hurriedly before Chloë caught on.

Mum knew I was up to something. She kept asking me what I was doing with my time, and seemed to know I wasn't spending my days with Chloë. Eventually, under her never-ending questioning, I gave in and fessed up.

'There's a boy I like,' I said, feeling my cheeks flame.

'I knew it!' she said in triumph. 'Does he like you?'

'I think so,' I said. 'We haven't – you know – done anything, but we get on really well.'

We'd been in the car at the time – I always found it easier to talk to Mum in the car, because then she couldn't fix me with her piercing stare. Now she glanced at me, briefly, before returning her attention to the road.

'There are some things you can do,' she said.

'Spells?'

'Well, yes, but not . . .'

I was cross.

'No,' I said firmly. 'No spells.'

Mum looked disappointed.

'No spells,' I said again. 'That's not how I want this to happen.'

When our exam results arrived, late that summer, I ran down the hill and along the shore to find Jamie. He was standing by the entrance to the cave, flushed with success and holding his own brown envelope.

'All As!' I bellowed as I hurtled towards him.

'Me too!' he waved his envelope at me.

He grabbed me round the waist and hugged me hard. Startled at such a display of physical affection, I stiffened, then suddenly realising I liked it, I let myself relax into his arms. For such a lanky boy he was surprisingly muscular. Shocked at my confidence, I ran my hands along his back and laced my fingers through his soft wavy hair.

'I couldn't have done it without you, Esme,' he muttered into my shoulder. Then he lifted his head and looked at me. And slowly, he bent forward and kissed me.

Chapter 14

Now I shivered with pleasure remembering that first kiss as I stood in the shower. I'd kissed a couple (well, OK, a lot) of men since then but very few had lived up to the thrill of my first snog.

Climbing out of the shower I wrapped myself in a towel and went into my bedroom to get dressed. Sitting on the bed I pulled my bedside cabinet drawer out all the way. There, pinned to the back and hidden from prying eyes, was a photo of Jamie. Smiling in disbelief that it was still there, I pulled it off and stared at it.

Jamie was laughing, standing on the shore of the loch, his eyes screwed up against the summer sun. It was taken just before he'd gone off to boarding school for sixth form.

After we'd got our exam results, we'd spent the rest of the summer curled up in the cave snogging until our lips ached. I'd told Chloë every detail of our romance, but I'd kept Jamie a secret from Mum and when he'd asked me to meet his parents I'd made excuse after excuse. I wanted to keep him separate from the rest of my life and I certainly didn't want him to meet my oddball family or experience any of the strange things that happened in our house. So, although he knew my family ran the café, I never took him there or met him anywhere besides the cave. I spent the whole summer veering madly from agony to ecstasy and back again, loving being with Jamie and terrified he'd find out the truth, and dump me.

What happened, though, was worse. I'd told mum when Jamie and I became officially a couple and she'd looked very pleased with herself. But even then I hadn't thought she'd had anything to do with it. Until I came home one day. It was the summer bank holiday and we'd had a great day. Me, Chloë, Jamie and Chloë's new boyfriend Frankie – a Scottish Italian boy with the most beautiful dark skin and eyes – had been to the fair in Inverness. I came home feeling queasy from too much candyfloss and one too many goes on the dodgems.

Frankie was older than us and could drive, so he dropped me off. I'd lost my door key – again – and knew Mum would be cross when she found out, so I scaled the side gate, then quietly let myself in the back door. The house was deserted and I was pleased. I planned to curl up on the sofa and read for a while until my queasiness went away. I ran upstairs and picked up my book, then headed for the lounge. But as I walked past Mum's room, I heard her muttering inside – and among the whispers I heard her say my name. Intrigued, I paused and listened. She said it again. Then I heard her say 'Jamie' and I knew, suddenly, what she was doing.

Furious, I flung open the door. Mum was sitting on the floor surrounded by pink flowers and holding my favourite top, and my well-thumbed copy of *Pride and Prejudice*.

I looked at her in horror.

'What are you doing?' I said, though I knew what she was doing. It was obvious. She was doing a love spell. And by her guilty expression, I was pretty convinced it wasn't the first time she'd done one. It was like the scales fell from my eyes and I saw myself as I really was – an awkward, ungainly teenager who a boy like Jamie would never want to be with, unless my meddling mother cast a spell to make him fall for me.

'Esme,' Mum said. 'I can explain . . .'

But I didn't stay to find out what her explanation was. In

68

despair I turned and fled, sobbing as I went. I was heartbroken and embarrassed and betrayed and I couldn't bear it. Crying great big wrenching sobs – I don't think I've ever cried like that before or since – I shut myself in my room and threw some bits in a bag. Then when my tears had finally subsided, I went downstairs to find Mum.

She was sitting at the kitchen table, cup of tea at her elbow, looking white and worried.

'Can I have a lift to Inverness?' I said.

'Esme, darling, I just want you to understand what I was doing . . .'

But I didn't want to hear her excuses. I felt sick just thinking about it.

'I can't talk about it, Mum,' I said. 'I'm going to see Harry.' I hadn't spoken to Harry but I knew she wouldn't turn me away. We were good friends back then, despite the age difference.

Mum knew when she was beaten. She got up and picked up her car keys.

'I'll take you to the station,' she said. 'But we need to talk about this. I have to explain.'

I shook my head.

'No,' I almost shouted. 'I won't listen.'

I waved my hand over my head. Pink sparks showered down on my shoulders and Mum looked shocked.

She moved her mouth but it sounded like my ears were full of cotton wool.

'I can't hear you,' I said. 'I can't hear anything you're saying. I can cast spells too.'

We drove to Inverness in silence – I could hear everything except Mum's voice – and I went to Harry's. But, like I said, she let me down too. And so, feeling alone and sad and betrayed, I rang my dad – I had been a bit of a Daddy's girl back then, still was, and I always turned to him in a crisis – and asked if I could stay with him for a while.

'Actually Ez,' he said. 'I've been thinking about that. We're friendly with a chap here, I play cricket with him, who's head-master of a school nearby. It's a good school, with lots of academic success.'

'OK,' I said. I couldn't understand why Dad's social life had anything to do with me and I didn't care less about the cricket team.

'There's a place there for you if you want it,' he said. 'You can board during the week and come home to Olivia and me at weekends. I think it would be good for you, Esme.'

Suddenly it all seemed easy. I would leave Claddach and go to Cheltenham. Leave behind Mum and Suky, Harry, and – I could barely even think of him – Jamie. Poor Jamie who would no doubt have found himself a much more suitable girlfriend if Mum hadn't stuck her nose in and forced him to kiss me instead. If I was out of the picture, he'd be free to move on.

After that, things moved quickly. Dad called Mum and they talked about the logistics. I could tell from Mum's face that she was upset when Dad explained, but though my spell was wearing off it hadn't gone completely and I was still finding it pretty hard to hear her. I met up with Chloë and told her what had happened and where I was going. She was upset of course, but she was totally in love with Frankie and was a bit distracted.

And Jamie. That was the tricky bit. He didn't have long before school started – I had longer because the English schools went back later, but I wanted to get to Cheltenham as soon as possible. I couldn't bear to be in Claddach for a second longer than I had to be. I'd avoided Jamie for the rest of the weekend while I'd been at Harry's, but I knew I had to face him and tell him I was going.

Except I didn't. Instead, I wrote him a letter telling him I was off to school in England and that I thought we should call things off. Of course, I didn't mention that my mum had cast a love spell and now I would never know if he'd have fallen for me without it. I wrote a lot of guff about moving on and devoting ourselves to our studies. I made an empty promise to keep in touch 'as friends' but I didn't put Dad's address on the top, and even changed my number. How terrible was that? Even now, a decade later, I felt ashamed when I thought about how shabbily I handled our break-up and how cowardly I was.

Despite my attempts to disappear, Jamie got my new address – at school and at Dad's – from Mum I assume. He wrote a few times, but I didn't reply and eventually his contact ceased. I was relieved when his letters stopped, but sad as well, and I often thought about the fun we'd had on that last weekend we'd spent together. How much fun we'd had that whole summer, really. I suppose things always look sun-kissed and idyllic when you're looking back, but Jamie and I had the most perfect romance that summer. We sat on the beach and talked for hours, we hung out with Chloë and Frankie, we went on days out together – one particularly hilarious trip ended with Jamie plunging into a river after he tried to clamber out of our hired canoe and ended up with his arms on the bank and his feet in the boat. He stretched out like a cartoon character, and then gave up and dived into the murky – freezing – water. I laughed until I cried. The whole summer was like that. We were just really, really happy. Until Mum stuck her nose in and it all went wrong.

Chapter 15

I looked at the photo in my hand. Jamie would be twenty-eight now, too. I wondered what he'd be like. Very grown up I imagined. He was a doctor now. I couldn't even imagine it. Chloë – who'd gone to Edinburgh University at the same time as him – shared a few mutual friends, so she'd filled me in on a few snippets of information about him every now and then. In fact, the last thing she'd told me was that he'd got engaged to another doctor. I touched his sixteen-year-old face in the photograph gently, wondering if our paths would cross while I was in Claddach. It seemed inevitable if he was looking after Suky and I felt a bit sick just thinking about it. What would I say to him?

Carefully I pinned the photo back where it had been and replaced the drawer just as my phone rang, startling me out of my memories. It was Dom.

'Hello, sweetheart,' he said. 'How's things?'

Pleased to hear from him, I filled him on Suky's treatment and what Chloë was up to. He told me about some office politics that were annoying him and mentioned he'd been out drinking on Friday night.

'Who was there?' I asked. I wasn't really interested but thought I should pretend.

'Oh you know, the usual,' Dom said airily. 'Liz, Mike, Patrick,' he named some lawyers from his department, then added overly-casually, 'Oh that new trainee was there too. Vicky I think her name is.'

I knew Vicky. She was young and ambitious and it seemed she'd certainly caught Dom's attention. He mentioned her at least another three times in our short conversation – apparently Vicky had seen some West End show that everyone was talking about, and she'd been amazing in a meeting, and she'd told some funny story . . .

We chatted some more and then I hung up. Hating myself for feeling suspicious, I pondered Dom's manner when he mentioned Vicky. He was hiding something, I thought, and not hiding it very well. They'd obviously been spending time together. Perhaps she'd made a move on him or maybe he thought she was hot; she was a pretty girl with a great figure that was certain. I looked at myself in the mirror as I brushed my hair. And she was at least five years younger than me, I thought miserably. And I was five years younger than Rebecca, a voice whispered in the back of my mind.

I didn't trust Dom, I suddenly realised, sweeping my hair up into a ponytail. And that wasn't too surprising considering I knew for a fact he was a cheat. The thought made me shudder.

Chapter 16

I wiped down the table gloomily. It was 8am on Monday morning and the café was deserted. Rain lashed at the windows and I would rather have been snuggled up in my Take That duvet than squirting anti-bac on to tables. Behind me, Nell, the café's waitress, was arranging cakes precisely on the counter. I glanced at her in admiration. I wouldn't have been so eager to give my free periods up when I was sixteen.

'I need the money,' Nell said, reading my mind. 'And I like working here.' She positioned a slice of carrot cake neatly with her long skinny fingers and smiled at me broadly.

'Eva has been very good to me,' she said. 'I had a bit of trouble at school and stuff and she got Suky to give me a tonic to help me get my confidence back."

Another 'tonic'. I smiled half-heartedly. I couldn't imagine how Nell had lost her confidence – she was gorgeous with floppy dark hair down to her shoulders. She was wearing a baggy jumper that slipped artfully off one shoulder, a very short denim skirt, bare legs (it was freezing!) and cowboy boots. She looked great. I was in jeans that were already a bit snug thanks to too many muffins (it was hard being in a café all day without nibbling) and a jumper I'd borrowed from Mum. I felt scruffy and out of sorts.

Behind me the café door opened, tinkling the bell that had hung over the hinges for years. I ignored it. Let Nell deal with customers. It was much more her forte than mine and besides, it was far too early for me to be making small talk.

'Morning, Doc,' Nell called. "You're up and about early.'

'House calls,' a voice replied. A shiver ran down my spine and I froze, damp cloth in hand. If I just stand very still and stay here, I thought, maybe he won't notice me.

'Esme,' Nell said cheerfully. 'Come and meet our local lifesaver.'

I swore under my breath and fixed a smile to my face. Then I turned round and walked, very slowly, past the empty tables to where he stood.

'Dr James Brodie,' Nell said. 'Meet Esme McLeod. She's Tess's daughter.'

He was older, of course, but he hadn't changed that much. He'd filled out and his brown eyes had thin lines around them. But his hair was still tousled like a little boy's and he had the same crooked smile.

Jamie stared straight at me and held out his hand politely.

'It's a pleasure to meet you,' he said.

My stomach was filled with butterflies, all flapping their wings madly.

'We've met,' I said softly, looking at my feet.

Nell laughed delightedly. 'Of course! You must be about the same age. Did you go to school together?' she said. Neither of us answered her. She looked from me to Jamie and frowned.

'Do you remember Esme?' she asked Jamie.

'Not really.' Jamie watched me carefully. I stared back, determined not to react.

Nell looked puzzled. She glanced at me and I shook my head gently, hoping she'd get the message. She did. 'I'd, er, better get on,' she said and scurried into the kitchen.

I cleared my throat.

'What can I get you?' I said brightly. 'Tea with no sugar is it?'

Jamie ignored my question. 'You came home then?' he said. 'After all this time.'

I nodded.

'It's been a while,' I said nervously.

'A while?' Jamie sat down on one of the café's wooden chairs and stared at me. It made me feel very uncomfortable. I pulled out a chair and sat down opposite him, feeling like I was in a job interview.

'So you've taken over from your dad,' I began. I pleated the damp dishcloth between my fingers and waited for Jamie to reply. He didn't.

Wrinkling my nose, I took a deep breath and started again, hoping I could melt his steely heart. 'Anyway. I heard you didn't stick around either.'

'Been keeping tabs on me, have you?' he asked. I looked up at him, hoping he was smiling, but he wasn't.

I blushed.

'Chloë mentions you, every now and then,' I said. 'I was surprised to hear you were back, I thought you'd be off saving the world somewhere.'

Jamie nodded.

'Tried it,' he said with a sheepish smile. 'Didn't really like it. Decided I could save the world just as well from here.'

'So now you're home,' I said.

'And so are you,' Jamie pointed out. He sounded resigned, as though my being in Claddach at the same time as him was the worst possible scenario. He probably had a point.

'It's not permanent,' I said quickly. I didn't want him thinking I was back for good. 'But yes, for now, I'm home.' I shook out my dishcloth and began folding it into a square.

'Cup of tea was it?'

As I made Jamie's tea I fought the urge to shake him and shout, 'It wasn't my fault!' I had no clue that he'd still be so upset about it all, ten years on, and I felt cross at Mum all over again for putting me in such an awkward position. Again.

I sneaked a look at him as he sat waiting for his cuppa. He was still good-looking. I wondered where his fiancée was. Probably performing open-heart surgery while cooking a gourmet meal and running a marathon. That was the sort of girl he'd always deserved – not a loser witch with unruly hair and a problem with commitment like me.

I gave him his tea and he handed over the money.

'Oh there's no need,' I began, but he waved me away.

'Thank you,' he said in an uber-polite fashion. 'See you around.'

He turned and left. I watched him go, wondering if things would always be odd between us. Probably. If I'd been in his position, I wouldn't want to forgive and forget either.

I was startled out of my reverie by a group of hikers who arrived to pick up a packed lunch. Nell sorted it out with impressive speed and sent them on their way with a cheery wave.

As the door shut behind them, I looked at her.

'That was the most customers I've seen in here since I came back,' I said.

She sat down on one of the sofas by the window.

'I know,' she said. 'Things are not good.'

'Do you know why?'

'I've got an idea,' she said, watching me closely. 'Do you know why?'

'I've got an idea,' I said.

We stared at each other for a minute. I didn't know if she knew the truth about Mum, Suky and Eva and I cursed myself for not thinking to check with Mum before I'd started my shift.

Nell looked around her. I didn't know why she bothered; the café was deserted.

'Promise you won't say anything to Suky?'

I nodded.

'I think she made some mistakes,' Nell said. Her pretty face was grave. 'I think she gave out some tonics that didn't work and now I think some people are talking.'

It was so exactly what Suky had said that I almost gasped.

'People?' I said.

'I think it's the Housewives' Guild,' she whispered, even though there was no one around to hear her. 'Millicent Fry and her cronies.'

'The one with the hat?' I was whispering too.

Nell nodded. She pushed her sleeves up and I caught a glimpse of some silvery white scars on her forearms. She saw me look and pulled her jumper down again.

'I saw Millicent snogging the face off her husband a few weeks ago,' she said. 'It was disgusting. And like completely not what she does. I reckon Suky totally had a hand in that.'

I gulped, not sure whether to fess up on Suky's behalf.

'Even if Suky didn't make Millicent fruity, she's definitely involved,' Nell continued. 'She loves a drama. Other people's misfortunes are her lifeblood.'

I raised my eyebrows. That sounded a bit over the top to me.

'I know her daughter, Imogen,' Nell explained.

'Are you friends?'

'Have you seen *Mean Girls*?'

'Ah,' I understood. 'Is Imogen one of the "mean girls" at your school?'

'Totally,' Nell said. 'She's poisonous. And I reckon her mum is just as bad.'

'Maybe,' I said. I made a mental note to watch out for this Millicent and to see if I could find out anything about the Housewives' Guild. Could those harmless middle-aged women really be the cause of the café's troubles?

Funnily enough, after such a gloomy chat with Nell, the café got a bit busier. There were a few groups of walkers wanting lunch, along with some tourists and two elderly women who told me they were on a painting holiday. I told them all about Eva's husband, Allan, and proudly sent them off in the direction of his studio to have a look at his work.

Chapter 17

Later in the afternoon, the bell jingled and Brent came in.

He strode up to the counter and flashed me his blinding smile.

'Esme!' he said. 'I was hoping to see you – how is Suky? Will she be needing a lift tomorrow?'

Like before, his over-exuberance made me feel sulky and sullen, but I knew he was doing us a big favour, so I plastered a smile on.

'Her cold isn't as bad as we thought,' I said. 'So she should be fine to go again tomorrow – if you don't mind.'

Nell appeared at my elbow, her face flushed and her eyes sparkling. I looked at her suspiciously. Did she have a crush on the handsome Yank?

'That's very kind of you,' she said. 'Isn't it kind of him, Esme?'

'It's very kind,' I said, worrying I was going to sound sarcastic when I really didn't mean to be. 'He's a very nice man.'

Brent flashed me his smile again.

'Drop me a text later and let me know when you want me to come get you. Will it be you going with her again?'

'It will be, actually,' I said, not sure if that was good or bad.

'Great,' Brent said. 'I was hoping you'd say that.'

We looked at each other awkwardly for a moment.

'Well, Esme McLeod, I have some work to do,' he said. 'Could I trouble you for an herbal tea?' He pronounced it 'urbal'.

'Cake?' said Nell.

'I shouldn't,' he said. 'But I will. One of those flapjacks, please.'

He took the plate and went to sit by the window where he got a laptop out of his bag and was soon deep in concentration.

'He is gorgeous!' Nell hissed at me as I dumped a chamomile teabag in a pot. 'He makes me go a bit funny.' She gazed adoringly at Brent, who was oblivious to her attention, and typing fast, his fingers flying across the keys.

'He likes you,' she said.

I put the pot on a tray and added a mug.

'No he doesn't,' I said. I gave her the tray. 'You serve him.'

Nell looked aghast at the suggestion.

'Nooooo,' she squealed, shoving the tray back at me. 'I can't. I'm too flustered. I'll drop something.'

With an over-exaggerated sigh I took the tray.

'OK then,' I said. 'But you're missing your chance here.'

Nell laughed and took up position at the end of the counter where she could watch Brent without worrying he might talk to her. I went over to the window and put the tray down on Brent's table.

He glanced up at me.

'What's upstairs?' he said.

Surprised by his question, I frowned in confusion.

'Oh sorry,' he said. 'I was just wondering. From outside you can see there are windows but there are no stairs in here.'

'Oh,' I said, understanding what he meant. 'There's a staircase out the back. It's just junk up there really. Great views across the loch, though.'

He nodded.

'Must be,' he said. 'Must be.'

He bowed his head to his computer again and I crept away.

Brent stayed about an hour, then left with yet another beaming smile telling me he couldn't wait to see Suky and me tomorrow. By the time he went home, there were no customers left, giving me plenty of time to brood over Jamie and how horrible things had been. Eventually, Mum called.

'Harry's on her way,' she said. 'Shut up early and come home – we'll have a nice family dinner.'

Brilliant. What a perfect ending to a perfect day. But I couldn't say no, so Nell and I cleaned up what little mess there was, switched off the lights and locked up. Then together we walked up the path towards town.

As we approached the road where we'd go our separate ways, Nell clutched my arm.

'There's Millicent,' she said. 'With Imogen and her brother Bradley.'

I looked over. Millicent was standing at the bus stop – still wearing her tartan hat – with two beautiful blonde teenagers.

'Are they twins?' I asked Nell, who was trying very hard to hide behind me.

'Yep,' she said. 'Twice as evil as normal people.'

Given my own mother was a twin, I thought that was a bit unfair, but I didn't disagree. As we watched, the bus drew up and the twins got on. Millicent waved them off, then began walking towards us.

'Hello, lassies,' she said in a cut-glass Home Counties English accent. I stifled a giggle.

'Hello, Mrs Fry,' Nell said. 'This is Esme McLeod.'

'Och, Esme!' Millicent said. 'I've heard a lot about you.'

'And I you,' I said politely.

'You must be thrilled to be home,' she said, rolling her Rs like Mrs Doubtfire. 'You must miss the Old Country when you're not here.'

'Scotland,' Nell said, helpfully. 'She means Scotland.'

'Erm,' I said. 'I like London.'

'But it's not a patch on here, though, eh?' She took a deep breath. 'The air. The scenery. I look on Scotland as my homeland now.'

'I can see that,' I said, not sure what to make of her.

'Now tell me,' she said companionably. 'How is Suky doing?'

'She's OK,' I said.

I thought a shadow crossed her face, though it could have just been the brim of her tam o' shanter.

'Give her my love,' she sang. 'Awfully nice to meet you, Esme.'

I watched her bustle away towards the B&B then Nell and I collapsed in giggles.

'She seems harmless,' I said, unable to think that anyone in a hat like that could be a threat.

Nell snorted. 'That's what she wants you to think,' she said. 'Just don't be fooled.'

I wasn't sure, but I promised Nell I'd keep an eye on her and we said goodnight.

Chapter 18

Wearily I made my way up the hill wondering if Harry was home yet. I had cake crumbs in my hair and coffee down my shirt, and I wanted a chance to get myself together before I saw her. But of course I didn't get the chance. As I let myself in the front door I heard a burst of laughter from the kitchen. Harry was obviously home and being very entertaining.

I paused at the bottom of the stairs, wondering if I could sneak up and grab a shower before anyone realised I was there. I put my foot on the bottom step.

'Ez,' Harry called from the kitchen. Damn her and her aura reading – she'd have known I was there from the second I'd opened the door. 'Come and have a drink.'

I glanced in the hall mirror, noting my shiny face and messy hair with dismay, then dived into my bag for my hairbrush. Quickly I pulled it through my curls before twisting them up out of the way. I daubed on some lip gloss and pulled Mum's old jumper off over my head to reveal a fitted T-shirt I'd been wearing as a vest. Slightly better.

I pushed open the kitchen door. Harry was there, leaning against the counter with a glass of wine in her hand. Her cheeks were flushed and her eyes a bit too bright. I wondered if she'd been crying – it looked like she might have been, though I couldn't remember the last time I'd seen my cousin shed a tear.

'Hi, Harry,' I said. I blew her a kiss from where I stood – easier than giving her one for real, then I hugged Suky, who was sitting at the table drinking fizzy water next to Mum who was drinking the same wine as Harry.

'You look a bit better,' I said to Suky. 'How's the cold?'

'Not bad at all,' she said. 'Dr B says I can go back to radio-therapy tomorrow – it's all arranged.'

I shuddered at the mention of Jamie, but tried not to show my discomfort.

'I'll text Brent then,' I said, sitting down too and pulling my phone out of my pocket. Quickly I sent the message, as Eva and Allan piled through the back door waving another bottle of wine.

'Hello, chuck,' Eva said, folding Harry into a huge hug. Behind her back, Allan waved the wine bottle at me.

'Fancy a glass, Ez?'

'Yes please,' I said, pushing my chair back.

'Don't get up,' Mum said. 'You've been on your feet all day.' She waved her hand and the cupboard door flew open and out floated three glasses. One landed in front of me, the others in front of Allan and the chair where Eva was about to sit. Then the cork popped out of the bottle and neatly, the bottle tipped and poured itself into our glasses.

'Cheers,' said Eva. She clinked her glass against mine.

'Cheers,' I said, far less cheerily.

Harry sat down next to me.

'Cheer up, misery guts,' she said. 'Tell us about this Brent.'

I filled her in on how Suky and I had met him – leaving out the bit about my hopeless attempt at mending the car – and told her he seemed nice, if a bit annoying.

'He could be the man for you,' Harry said, winking at me. 'Sounds perfect.'

I made a face at her.

'Where's Natalie?' I said, suddenly realising Harry's girlfriend wasn't part of our gathering.

'In America,' Harry said. 'She's got some family stuff on.'

Her face was unreadable but I got the definite impression she didn't want to talk about Nat. That was weird. They'd been together since Harry had done her Masters in the States years ago and, though Natalie wasn't a witch herself, she was a regular fixture at McLeod family events. More regular than me, in fact.

Sensing an atmosphere, Mum clapped her hands.

'Who's hungry?' she said. Suky made a face – she'd lost her appetite since starting treatment – but Eva, Harry and Allan all agreed they were starving.

'Shall we get a take-away?' I asked. 'I saw some menus by the front door. Indian? Chinese?'

Harry laughed.

'Bless you, Ez,' she said. 'We can do better than that.' She waggled her fingers and silvery sparks flew round the kitchen. Even her colours were better than mine, I thought glumly. Everyone's colours were better than mine actually – my pink sparks were twee and hard to disguise. Harry and Suky's silvery shimmers could be passed off as a heat haze, Mum's cloudy grey sparkles often looked like a trick of the light, and Eva's earthy brown glitter was simply beautiful.

Suddenly the table was full of food – curries smelling delicious, warm scented naans and crispy poppadoms.

'Well done, Harry,' Eva cried, pointing over her head with a flourish and making plates appear in front of everyone. There was a real celebratory atmosphere even though the reason we were all together – the fact that Suky had cancer – was not happy and I was like the spectre at the feast. I just couldn't loosen up enough to enjoy myself properly. I was worried about Jamie and the empty tables in the café, though thanks to Eva and Allen's presence I felt less awkward around Mum and Harry.

'I am stuffed,' said Harry a while later, pushing her plate away.

She'd polished off an enormous amount of curry, despite her skinny frame. I didn't know where she'd put it.

'Are you OK, Ez?' Mum said. I had eaten barely anything, pushing my chicken tikka round my plate.

'Fine,' I said. 'I'm just tired.'

Harry looked at me sharply and I pushed all thoughts of Jamie out of my head. I didn't want her poking around in my thoughts uninvited.

'How's the café?' she said instead. 'Are you doing OK with your magic?'

'Not bad,' I said. 'I'm rusty though. I've been trying to read my spell book but I keep falling asleep.'

Harry waggled her fingers over the dishes and they all rose from the table and stacked themselves in the dishwasher.

Then she leaned across the table and took my hand.

'I need a project,' she said. 'Let me give you a refresher.'

'Oh no,' I said. 'No, no, no.' The one thing worse than doing magic was doing it under Harry's guidance.

'It's not a bad idea,' Suky said. 'It will be nice for you two to spend some time together.'

'No,' I said again. I waggled my own fingers in the direction of the wine bottle. It flew across the table and poured a neat, wineglass-amount of liquid right next to where my glass actually was.

As one, Harry, Mum, Suky and Eva looked at the puddle of wine on the table then up at me.

'Go on,' Harry said. 'Please.'

I was wavering. It was certainly true that I needed help with my magic. But if Harry was back then she could be the Third.

'I've got some stuff going on,' Harry said, her bottom lip quivering. 'Helping you would really take my mind of it all.'

I looked at her suspiciously, knowing from bitter experience of childhood battles that she could cry on demand, but Mum, Suky and Eva all melted.

'Go on,' Mum said. 'You could do with a bit of a refresher.'

'Where would we do it?' I said. 'There's not enough room in the house. Magic lessons – especially where I was concerned – really needed space.'

'My studio,' Allan said. Disloyal, evil Allan. 'I'm off to Glasgow tomorrow for a few days. You can have the run of the place. There's loads of room.'

I knew when I was beaten.

'OK,' I said. 'Fine. But if you're mean to me, the lessons stop.'

Harry laughed.

'Oh Esme,' she said in a baby voice. 'When have I ever been mean to you?'

Suky stood up.

'I'm whacked,' she said. 'I'm off to bed.'

Harry got up too. She picked up her Mulberry handbag from the back of the chair and rooted about inside it.

'Night, Mum,' she said. She gave Suky a hug. She towered over her mum and her olive skin and dark hair stood out next to Suky's freckled arms and blonde bob. Not for the first time I wondered if Harry's mysterious dad had been Indian. Suky never talked about him but she had met him while she was in Delhi, so it was possible. As I pondered my cousin's parenthood, a sudden movement caught my eye. Had she just passed something to Suky? It had looked like a small square parcel. But I couldn't see anything now – perhaps I'd imagined it. It was late and I'd been drinking. Maybe I was hallucinating now.

'I'm going up too,' I said. I was worn out. Magic hung, heavily, over the table and my head ached with the pressure of it all.

I climbed the stairs slowly thinking about magic lessons, radio-therapy, Jamie and Dom. But as I passed Suky's room, I paused. Her door was closed and the room was dark, but under the door I thought I could see a few faint sparks, as though she was doing magic. I blinked and looked again and they were gone.

'Time for bed,' I thought, pulling on my pyjamas. 'Thank goodness today is over.'

Chapter 19

'I just don't understand why you don't want to go,' I said to Harry the next morning. I had assumed – wrongly as it turned out – that she would want to accompany her mum to the hospital that day.

'I've got some stuff to do,' she said. We were standing in the hall and she was doing her make-up in the large mirror by the front door. She looked, as always, well-put-together and elegant. I avoided my own reflection, knowing my hair would be a tousled mess and my own unmade-up face ruddy and tinged with grey thanks to last night's wine and curry.

'Work stuff?'

I was standing behind her, but I could see her face in the mirror. She looked cagey.

'Some work stuff, yes. And some other bits Mum asked me to do.'

I wasn't convinced. Harry had a talent for wriggling out of unpleasant tasks purely because she didn't fancy them.

'Please, Ez,' she said. 'If you can go with Mum this morning, then I'll start your magic lessons this afternoon.'

'Oh whoop-dee-bloody-doo,' I said. But I never could say no to Harry. 'Fine,' I said. 'But you're going tomorrow – Suky wants you there.'

Harry had the grace to look embarrassed. She paused in brushing her shiny hair and caught my eye in her reflection.

'I know,' she said. 'And I will go. I've just really got to get some stuff together.'

I frowned at her.

'Is this anything to do with the package you gave your mum last night?'

Harry bent at the waist to scoop her hair up into a knot.

'I didn't give Mum anything,' she said into her knees. I knew she was lying, but I didn't pursue it because Suky came downstairs. Radiotherapy was taking it out of her. She looked pale and thin and she had purple smudges under her eyes.

'Brent's on his way,' I said. 'Are you OK?'

She nodded.

Harry straightened up and studied her mum carefully.

'Have you eaten anything?' she said.

'I can't stomach anything,' Suky said. 'I've not felt this sick since I was expecting you.'

Harry gave a half-smile.

'Well, look how well that turned out,' she said. She flung an arm around Suky's shoulders and hugged her tightly. I watched, envying their easy friendship.

From outside, a car horn sounded.

'That'll be Brent,' I said. 'Let's go.'

Suky kissed Harry and – I thought – whispered something in her ear, but I couldn't be sure. Then we walked down the path and I helped her into the back seat of the Range Rover. She put on her seatbelt, leaned her head against the window and fell asleep almost immediately. I climbed into the passenger seat and exchanged a worried glance with Brent.

'She's feeling it, huh?' he said as he pulled away from the kerb.

'Seems to be,' I said. 'It's horrible to watch.'

Brent took his hand off the wheel and briefly gripped my fingers. The car was so big he had to lean across to reach me.

'It's all for a reason,' he said. 'Just try to remember that.'

I smiled at him, then pulled my hand away. We were more comfortable with each other now, but I still didn't feel we were at the touching stage. I could hear Nell's voice in my head, telling me Brent liked me and I didn't want any confusion about what kind of relationship we had, even though I still thought Nell was wrong.

We drove on in silence for a while.

'How are things at the café?' Brent said eventually.

'Oh fine,' I said.

'It's kind of quiet.'

'Time of year,' I said. 'And the weather's not great.'

He looked over at me.

'Really?'

I stared through the windscreen.

'No,' I admitted. 'Not really. It's been very quiet since I got back – and before, by all accounts.'

'Any idea why?'

'Does there have to be a reason?'

Brent slowed down as we approached the outskirts of Inverness.

'I've just heard a few things, that's all,' he said. 'Things that I don't think are fair, and I want you to know about.'

I felt sick. Was Nell's theory about Millicent and her Housewives' Guild right?

'What kind of things?' I whispered, looking into the back seat to check Suky was still asleep.

'Crazy stuff,' Brent said. He laughed but I got the impression he didn't think it was very funny.

'I've got quite friendly with some of the women in town, you know the ones,' he said. I closed my eyes, and nodded.

'They're always bringing me food, man,' he said. 'I don't know how they think I've lasted this long without their pies.'

I didn't speak. I just wanted him to get to the point.

'Anyway, I went along to one of their meetings yesterday, to chat to them about some tech stuff. And I overheard a few of their conversations.'

It was his turn to look into the back seat.

'They were talking about Suky,' he said. 'Implying she was messing with stuff she had no business messing with.'

'Like what?' I said.

Brent flinched at my sharp tone. 'I'm just telling you what I heard, Ez,' he said.

'Sorry,' I whispered. 'Go on.'

'Well, it sounds ridiculous but some of them were saying she had,' he gave a small chuckle, 'magical powers.'

I didn't laugh. Brent turned his head to look at me, like he was gauging my reaction, then turned back to the road.

'There seemed to be a view that she – and your Mum and their friend with the hair – were up to something,' he said. 'Something they didn't want to be a part of.'

So Suky had been right. Witches would be accepted while their spells worked, but if something went wrong, then woe betide us.

I forced myself to laugh.

'I've never heard anything so absurd in my whole life,' I said. 'Suky's a herbalist. Perhaps they're getting that confused with potions and cauldrons.'

Brent pulled into the hospital car park.

'Magical powers,' I said. 'I wish! It would help us find a parking space now, eh?'

As I spoke the car in the space in front of us pulled away, leaving the perfect gap for Brent to slot the Range Rover into. I glanced into the back seat. Suky's eyes were still closed but I got the distinct impression she was no longer asleep. So she could still manage a bit of magic, could she? Maybe I had seen sparks under her door last night after all.

I undid my seatbelt.

'Thank you for telling me,' I said to Brent, much more confidently than I felt. 'But I'm sure it's nothing, really. Business will pick up.'

We didn't discuss it again. Brent went back to Claddach and came to pick us up later. Suky felt so sick on the way home that I sat next to her, talking quietly all the way in an attempt to distract her. It was awful to see her suffer and I found myself blinking away tears, but I knew Brent had been right when he said it would be worth it in the end.

When we got home I was exhausted and emotional. I put Suky to bed, then I curled up on the sofa and fell asleep myself.

Chapter 20

An hour later I was woken by Harry.

'Come on, Ez,' she said, handing me a cup of tea. 'Let's get busy.'

Her eyes were sparkling. She really did love magic.

'Oh not today,' I said. 'I'm really not up for it. Anyway, I want to talk to you about the café.'

'Later,' she said. 'Mum's still asleep and Allan's gone – let's get down to his studio and get cracking.'

She was so excited I almost felt affectionate towards her.

'Come on, loser,' she said. Like I said. I almost felt affectionate. Almost.

I dragged myself off the sofa and followed her to Allan's studio, slurping at my tea as we walked through the garden.

Harry had been busy. She'd pushed all Allan's bits to the side and on the wooden floor of the studio she'd drawn a pentangle in chalk.

I looked at her.

'Is that really necessary?' I asked.

She shrugged.

'Probably not,' she admitted. 'But it'll give you something to focus on.'

I sat down on one side of the chalk drawing and she sat

opposite me. Allan's studio had originally been a garage so it was rectangular in shape with brick walls. He'd put in large windows all along one wall, and there were skylights above us. Normally the light flooded in, but now it had started to rain. I liked the sound of the drops hitting the glass.

Harry cleared her throat.

'Witchcraft is governed by certain rules,' she began.

'Is this going to take long?' I said. 'Only *Escape to the Country's* on in a minute.'

She glowered at me.

'Are you going to take this seriously?'

'Sorry,' I said. 'But I know all this. Don't harm anyone, anything you do will come back on you threefold, if you want something doing properly do it with three of you, blah blah blah.'

'Fine,' said Harry. 'Let's move on then.'

From behind her back she produced my spell book. I was annoyed.

'Have you been in my room?' I said.

Harry rolled her eyes.

'No, Esme,' she said. 'I haven't. I'm a witch. I can get stuff.'

She waved her hand in the air, and my pyjamas appeared, neatly folded, and plopped on to the floor next to me.

'Oh,' I said. 'Carry on.'

Harry flicked through the pages of my book.

'Look at this,' she said. 'Reams of stuff – spells, notes, ideas – all written by women just like you and me. McLeod women.'

I looked at the book.

'Some of it's written by me,' I said, recognising my childhood scrawl on one of the pages.

'Exactly,' Harry said. 'That's my point. It's in you, Esme. The magic's part of you. You can do it – you just need to remember how. God, when you were wee, you were always moving stuff and changing stuff just because you could.'

I blinked at her.

'Really?' I said. 'What sort of stuff?'

Harry smiled.

'My shoes, mostly,' she said. 'I locked them up in my wardrobe and you still got them.'

I did have a vague memory of tripping around in Harry's shoes when I was about six or seven.

'I had to lock them up with magic in the end,' she said, 'You were very cross.'

'I don't remember,' I said.

'Do you remember hiding Gran's keys?' Harry said. 'You did it all the time when you didn't want her to go out.'

'I do remember that,' I said. 'But I don't remember it being magical.'

'Well once you hid them in 1965,' Harry said. 'If that's not magic, I don't know what is. I never did work out how you'd done it.'

I stared at her, my mouth open in surprise. Had I really been such a competent witch when I was so young?

'It's all inside you, Ez,' Harry said. 'You've just hidden it for so long you've forgotten how to do it. Let it out.'

Suddenly I really, really wanted to learn.

'Go on then,' I said. 'What shall I do first?'

Harry put the spell book into the centre of the pentangle.

'Move this,' she said.

'Ooh it's like you're Yoda and I'm Luke Skywalker,' I said. 'There is no try . . .'

Harry silenced me with a look. I grinned at her. I could do this one.

I looked at the book and reached out to it with my mind. I could feel the edges of the pages, and the smooth leather of the cover in my head. Then I waggled my fingers and the book rose into the air surrounded by pink sparks.

'Ha!' I said.

'Not bad,' Harry said. But she wasn't done. All afternoon we worked. She had me lifting books, chairs, Allan's easel and, eventually, Eva's bike, which was leaning against the studio's outside wall, dripping in the rain.

Finally she clapped her hands.

'That's enough for today,' she said. 'Same time tomorrow?'

I yawned.

'No, that's all,' I said. 'I'm fine now. Thanks for your help.'

Harry wasn't having any of it.

'No way,' she said. 'We're only just starting. You've got a long way to go yet.'

She was right. Again. And I was annoyed with her for being right. Again.

Chapter 21

The next day Harry climbed into Brent's Range Rover with Suky while Mum went to the café so I had the morning to myself. I had big plans. I would go for a run, check my work emails, maybe paint my nails. What I actually did was sleep. All morning. Then I drowsily made myself a sandwich. As I lifted the bread to my mouth, my phone beeped with a text from Harry. *Meet me on the beach by the café in 10 minutes*, it said. Knowing it was useless to even argue, I swallowed my sandwich in two bites, threw on a jumper and jeans and headed for the beach.

Harry was sitting on a rock looking out across the loch. She looked like an album cover picture with her hair blowing in the breeze. I trudged across the shingle to meet her.

'Ready for round two?' she asked as I approached.

'As I'll ever be,' I said. 'What's on the agenda for today?'

'Today we're bringing things to us,' she said. She shivered. 'It's freezing out here.'

'I know,' I said. 'Why did you want to meet here anyway?'

Harry grinned.

'We need some other people,' she said. I felt nervous suddenly. I wasn't sure about involving strangers in my magic.

'But first,' Harry said, 'I need my hat.'

'Where is it?' I looked round.

'It's on the coat hook in the hall,' she said. 'Get it for me.'

'Get it yourself, you lazy cow,' I said.

Harry put her head in her hands.

'I despair,' she said, her voice muffled. 'There is no hope.'

Realisation dawned on me.

'Oh, you mean get it with magic?' I said.

Harry laughed.

'Yes please,' she said. 'Go on.'

I had no idea where to begin.

'It's on the coat hook,' Harry said again. 'Picture it, but in the witchy bit of your head.'

I knew what she meant, oddly enough. Like I'd done with the book, I reached out with my mind and felt her hat. I could feel the soft wool in my mind's fingers and then suddenly I could feel it in my actual fingers – and there it was.

'Excellent!' Harry said. She looked very pleased with herself. 'I knew you could do it.'

She had been right when she said that was just the beginning though. We spent the afternoon taking stuff from passers-by and returning it before they'd noticed. Hats, scarves, a ball, a handbag and once a skateboard belonging to Millicent Fry's beautiful teenage son. He went sprawling on to the pavement along the shore of the loch, the skateboard appeared for a second next to Harry and me and then reappeared next to the teenager's feet. Harry laughed and laughed and I was strangely pleased that I'd made her happy.

Then Jamie walked past. If he saw Harry and me sitting on the beach he made no sign of it.

'Ooh,' said Harry. 'Let's get his bag.'

I looked at her.

'His black bag?' I said. 'His *doctor's* bag? The one that's no doubt full of the important medicine he's been using to look after your mum?'

Harry looked a bit ashamed for almost the first time ever.

'Oh is that the GP?' she said. 'I suppose we should leave him alone.'

I let myself relax, pleased she hadn't cottoned on to the history between Jamie and me.

'Hang on,' she said. Bugger. 'Isn't he your ex? The one who caused all that drama?'

'No,' I said.

She looked at me.

'Yes,' I admitted.

I could feel her poking about in my mind, trying to get hold of how I was feeling. Irritated and desperate not to let her hear my thoughts, I shut her out.

'Oi, stop it,' I said, pulling down the virtual shutters in my memories. 'Get out of my head.'

'Well done,' she said, more pleased with my witchcraft than annoyed that I was spoiling her fun. But I could feel her eyes on me as I watched Jamie saunter past us and up towards town.

'I've always felt a bit guilty about that,' she said, digging her toes into the dirty sand. The concept of Harry feeling guilty about anything was alien to me, so I turned to stare at her. She looked back at me, a small frown on her usually smooth forehead.

'About how I treated you when you came to see me,' she went on. 'I don't think I was as nice as I should have been.'

'You were a cow,' I said, remembering how crushed I'd been at her reaction.

'I was,' she admitted. 'Shall we head back now?' And that was as close to an apology as I was ever going to get from Harry.

Chapter 22

All week we worked on my magic – sometimes in Allan's studio and sometimes on the beach. I was exhausted, sleeping deeply and late into the morning on the days I didn't go with Suky to hospital. We covered charms, enchantments, cleansing rituals, spells to find things that were lost – just about everything in fact.

Eventually, five days after my intensive magic course had begun, Harry announced it was time for me to lead the enchanting of some of the cakes in the café. I was remarkably keen. I wanted Mum to see how far I'd come in just a few days, and I also wanted her to see I'd done it without her help.

'What do you need?' Harry asked, leaning over the counter and examining the cakes that were on display.

'We could do with some more of the creativity buns,' Mum said. They were one of the café's bestsellers – popular with the writers and artists who flocked to Claddach and found, mysteriously, that they produced their best work after a break for a cup of tea and a cake.

I was sitting on one of the tables. The café was empty and it was nearly closing time. Now I slid off on to me feet.

'Come on then,' I said. 'Let's get it over with.'

We gathered together and Mum produced a large bowl filled with the bun batter. She and Harry looked at me and I took a deep breath.

'I don't know what to say,' I said as I took their hands and they also clasped fingers.

'You do,' Harry said. 'Feel it.'

I closed my eyes and concentrated. Before I knew it my lips were moving and I was whispering words I didn't know I knew. I opened my eyes and watched pink sparks hover in the air, then fall into the batter mix.

Mum beamed at me.

'You did it,' she said. I beamed back, then remembered where I was and what I was doing.

'Well, don't get used to it,' I said. 'Now Harry's back and Suky's treatment is nearly over, I'm going to have to get back to London.'

Mum looked sad, and I felt slightly guilty.

'I'm not going yet,' I said hurriedly. 'Make use of me while you can. I'll close up. You two get up the road to see how Suky's doing.'

'Not so fast, McLeod,' Harry said. I made a face. I knew what was coming. She'd been giving me homework every evening to work on by myself. I thought she might have forgotten today's but no chance.

'One of the most powerful spells a witch can do concerns transfiguration,' she said, her voice dripping with drama. 'The art of turning something into something else.'

She felt in her pocket and pulled out a squishy rubber frog.

'This,' she said, 'is a dog toy.'

'I can see that,' I said. 'What are you doing with it?'

'I want you to turn it into a real frog,' she said. 'Now.'

She dropped the toy frog into my hand. I squeezed it and it croaked.

'Now?'

'Now.' She handed me a cake box. 'Put it in here when you're done and bring it up to the house.'

Mum was putting on her coat. She looked amused and impressed all at once.

'That's a tricky spell,' she said. 'Do you think she'll do it?'

'I'm here, Mum,' I said. 'How about asking me?'

She looked at me.

'Can you do it?'

I shook my head.

'I don't think so.'

Harry gave me a violent nudge that I thought was meant to be affectionate.

'Course you can,' she said. 'Come on, Auntie Tess, let's leave her to it.'

'Off you go then,' I said as they filed out of the door. 'I'll just stay here, by myself, and tidy up, and clean the loo, and turn things into frogs . . .'

But they'd gone. Outside, the evening had turned wild. The wind was whipping across the loch and black clouds were speeding across the sky. I plonked the frog on the counter, then I waggled my fingers and made the lights come on. Harry would be pleased.

I stared at the frog for a while, then I walked to the door that led to the toilets and waggled my fingers in that direction. I was secretly quite pleased that Harry's guidance meant I never had to clean a loo ever again. Then I cleaned the café tables the same way.

Jobs done, I lay down on one of the sofas and balanced the frog on my bent knees. I tried the first few words that came to mind, but nothing happened.

Closing my eyes, I tried reaching out with my mind. I could feel the frog's squidgy, beany body. I focused, breathing deeply, and felt it change under my imaginary fingers from rubber to damp, slimy frog skin. Bleurgh. I tried not to let my revulsion break my concentration. I felt my actual fingers tingle as sparks began to fly from them and I knew it was beginning to work. Just a few more minutes . . .

And then the café door tinkled and a voice cried, 'Hellooooo?'

Startled I leapt to my feet, sending the rubber frog flying. The sparks from my fingers twisted in mid air and shot towards the door where I was looking – towards Millicent Fry, who was standing in the doorway, a smile on her neat face.

'Oh, Esme,' she said. 'I wonder if you can help me . . .'

She stopped as my pink sparks hit her squarely in the chest.

'Oh,' she said in surprise. And then she disappeared.

'Shit, shit, shit,' I said. I almost vaulted the back of the sofa and ran to where moments before Millicent had been standing.

'Shit,' I said again. At my feet was a real, live, croaking frog. Wearing a tiny tam o' shanter. I'd bloody well turned Millicent Fry into a frog. And I had absolutely no idea what to do about it.

Quickly, I grabbed the cake box and tried to scoop the frog – Millicent – inside. It was harder than I'd thought it would be and for a while Millicent and I were involved in a rather undignified chase around the café. I have to say, she came out of it better than I did, as I scuttled across the floor on my hands and knees and she hopped elegantly away from me.

Eventually though, I threw myself at her with a dive a Premier League footballer would be proud of, gripped her in two hands and all but threw her into the box.

I closed the lid and held it shut.

'Millicent,' I whispered. 'I don't know if you can hear me, but I just want you to know I'm really sorry. I'm going to turn you back now.'

The frog croaked gently from inside the box.

I tried to reach out to it mentally, but nothing happened. Whatever the reason – stress, fatigue, just plain bad luck – I'd clearly exhausted my witchcraft quota for that day.

I fished my phone out of my apron pocket and rang Harry.

'H,' I said when she answered, using my childhood nickname for her without noticing. 'I've done something really, really silly.'

Once she'd stopped laughing, Harry was remarkably helpful.

She arrived less than ten minutes later, armed with my spell book and her own, and her iPad.

'There are some pretty good sites that might have a solution if we can't work it out,' she said, logging on to the café's Wi-Fi. I was astonished. Witchcraft really had moved on in the ten years since I'd rejected it.

I leafed through my spell book, but clearly none of my relatives were quite as stupid as me and there were no spells explaining how to turn someone back into a person if you'd accidentally turned them into a frog.

'Ah ha,' Harry said. 'I think this is the one. How's your French?'

'Is it in French?' I was in despair. Poor Millicent was doomed to stay small and green forever.

'Yes, unfortunately,' Harry said, swiping her iPad furiously. 'Oh no, hang on, here it is in English.'

'Right, go on then,' I said. I pushed the cake box towards her.

'No, you have to do it,' she said. She turned the iPad round so I could see the screen. It was a spells and charms website. Really. The internet was a marvellous thing.

I read the spell through once to myself. It seemed quite straightforward.

'I'll open the box,' Harry said. 'Then you can say the words.'

'OK,' I said. 'Let's go.'

Harry opened the lid and I looked in at the slightly sad-looking frog inside. Then I whispered the words from the iPad screen.

The lights in the café dimmed slightly as I spoke and I could feel the magic gathering over our heads, like a cloud.

There was a pink flash, and suddenly Millicent was standing in front of us. Her blonde curls were dishevelled and her tartan hat slightly askew.

Harry moved fast. She swept Millicent on to one of the chairs, and fixed an expression of concern on to her face.

'How are you feeling now, Mrs Fry?' she asked, taking one of Millicent's hands.

'What happened?' she said, looking confused. I felt sorry for her.

'You had a bit of a funny turn,' I said. That was an understatement. 'I was just closing up, you came in and started to speak, then you went a bit peculiar.'

Millicent was bewildered. Harry was talking softly under her breath, and stroking one of her hands. I didn't know what she was doing, but I could see the magic all around her.

'I feel OK,' Millicent said, sounding as surprised to say it as I was to hear it. 'In fact I feel absolutely fine.'

Harry grinned at her and dropped her hand.

'Great,' she said. 'What a relief. Thanks for popping in.'

Millicent got up, a wee bit unsteadily.

'I can't remember what it was I came in for,' she said.

'Oh dear,' Harry said. 'How strange. Do come back if you remember won't you?'

She steered her towards the door. Millicent still looked unsure.

'I don't remember anything,' she said.

Harry and I exchanged a look over Mrs Fry's head. So that's what my cousin had been doing while she held Millicent's hand. Crafty.

'You're probably just tired,' Harry said.

'Or hungry,' I added.

'You're so busy.' Harry opened the door.

'Go home and put your feet up,' I said. I picked up her scarf, which had obviously fallen off when she changed, and handed it to her. 'Come back soon.'

Millicent staggered out of the door and into the rainy evening. We watched her walk up the path, then I shut the door firmly and locked it.

'Shit,' I said. 'I think I've made things a whole lot worse for everyone.'

I made us both a coffee and explained what Brent had told me.

'He says the Housewives' Guild have been talking about us,' I said. 'He reckons he's heard crazy rumours about us.'

'But those crazy rumours could just be true,' Harry said. 'Mum did say she'd had a bit of trouble with a few spells.'

'And Millicent was the one whose spell turned her into a sex fiend,' I said.

'Kermit?' Harry said, her face creasing up in laughter again. 'Kermit was the one who was snogging her husband on the steps of the library?'

I giggled.

'Yes,' I said. 'That was her.'

I stopped laughing.

'What if she remembers what happened, H?' I said. 'What if she tells everyone?'

'She won't,' Harry said. I wished I could share her confidence. She looked at her coffee mug.

'We need a drink,' she said. 'Let's go to the pub.'

For once, I didn't argue.

Chapter 23

'My tummy hurts,' I complained as Harry put another drink in front of me later. I clutched my stomach dramatically and giggled.

She squeezed on to the bench beside me.

'Go on, move up,' she said, scooching along and squishing me into the wall. I shoved her back. Harry put her hand on my stomach and furrowed her brow. 'What seems to be the problem?' she asked in a pretend-serious voice.

I tried to look serious back. 'I think,' I said, swallowing a bubble of laughter, 'I think I've had too much vodka.' I hiccupped loudly and Harry dissolved in giggles again.

'Is this what your doctor boyfriend used to do?' she asked slyly.

I tried to frown at her, which was hard because I was having trouble controlling my eyebrows.

'He wasn't a doctor then,' I said. 'He was just a boy.'

'Awww,' Harry said. 'Just a boy, standing in front of a girl . . .'

'Shush,' I said urgently. 'I really need a wee.'

Sniggering, Harry moved over to let me out. I stood up, a bit shakily admittedly, and tried to walk in a straight line to the ladies. I could feel the regulars' eyes on me as I walked, so I attempted to look sober as I swayed towards the loo.

'Oof!' Suddenly I was face down on the floor with a mouthful of carpet. I blinked in surprise and spat out some fluff; luckily, I was far too drunk to feel any sort of embarrassment.

Hmm. It was quite nice to lie down. Maybe I could just stay where I was? I sniffed. Nope. The carpet smelled of old beer and mouldy shoes. I definitely had to get up. Right. Any minute now.

'Need a hand?'

At last! I grasped the large hand that was being offered and yanked myself upright. It was Jamie. I grinned at him.

'Helloooo!' I tried to give him a hug and toppled into him. He put his arm around me to steady me and I snuggled into his chest. Jamie picked a bottle top out of my hair.

'Having fun?'

'I am. I'm drunk.'

'I can see that.' Jamie waved at Harry over my head. 'Is that your cousin you're with? She looks a bit worse for wear, too.' Harry was slumping lower and lower in her chair, and her eyes were closing, but she was still laughing.

'Are you?' I looked up at Jamie. He was swaying slightly. No, that was me.

Jamie gently pushed me off his chest.

'No, I'm driving. I just popped in to see Maria.'

'Who's Maria?' I said crossly. I'd enjoyed resting against Jamie's wide chest.

Jamie pointed to the barmaid. 'That's Maria.'

I squinted at her. She had long glossy hair and she was very pretty. And very young.

'Why do you want to see her?'

'Why not?' Jamie shrugged. 'We're pals, that's all. She sometimes comes to rugby with me.'

I heaved myself up on to a bar stool and rested my elbows on the bar. At least I did eventually – they just kept slipping off.

'What does your fiancée think about you going to rugby with pretty ladies?' I asked, when I was finally stable. I took Jamie's coke out of his hand and drained the glass. 'I'm really thirsty.'

Jamie – very patiently – signalled to Maria to bring us another two drinks.

'I don't have a fiancée,' he said.

I frowned in confusion and patted his hand reassuringly.

'You do,' I explained earnestly. 'She's a doctor. Like you.'

Jamie rolled his eyes.

'I did have a fiancée. But we broke up last year.'

I was overcome with sorrow for poor lonely Jamie. My eyes filled with drunken tears.

'That's so sad,' I wailed. 'What happened?'

Jamie gave me a thin-lipped smile.

'Oh the usual. We grew apart. She wanted to work abroad and I wanted to come home. She's still working with the Red Cross as far as I know – think she's in Africa at the moment.'

I was impressed.

'Africa? That's very far away.'

Jamie nodded.

'She's in Tanzania, working with children . . .'

I'd lost interest because I'd just been struck with the most brilliant idea.

'Jamie!' I cried. 'I know what you need to do!' I leaned closer to him and lowered my voice to a loud whisper.

'Ask Maria out,' I bellowed.

'No.'

'Go on!'

'No.'

I was outraged.

'Why not?' I squinted at Maria across the bar. She was serving another customer and was trying very hard to ignore my interest.

'Look,' I pointed at her. 'She's lovely!'

'She is, as you say, lovely.'

'She's got nice hair, lovely figure, she's very, very pretty . . .'

Maria turned round to face me and I gasped.

'And she's Maria MacKenzie from school!'

Jamie laughed loudly.

'Do you know her?'

'Know her? No! But I know her big sister!' Once again I lowered my voice to what I thought was a quiet holler.

'She's very young you know.'

I gave Jamie a stern look.

'Don't take this the wrong way, but I think she's too young for you. What on earth were you thinking, asking her out?'

Jamie had given up and was snorting into his glass of coke, while Maria giggled nearby. I sensed it was time to leave. I felt unreasonably grumpy that Jamie was thinking about other women and I gave Maria an evil look across the bar. Now what had I been doing before Jamie so rudely interrupted me? Ah yes.

I staggered to the loo – what a relief – then back to Harry. She was curled up in the corner of the seat, snoring gently. I shoved her and she opened her eyes.

'I think we should go home,' she said.

'You're right.' I said. I pulled her upright and, with our arms wrapped round each other, we swayed, staggered and generally weaved our way back up the hill to the house. As we walked, my phone beeped with a message from Dom.

'Working late no fun without u,' it read. Pah. I threw my phone back into my bag.

'Who was that?' Harry asked as we let ourselves into the house, tiptoeing towards the kitchen in an over-exaggerated fashion.

Perhaps it was the vodka, or the fact that I'd spent more time with Harry in the last week than I had in the last decade, but I suddenly decided to tell her the truth.

I pulled out a chair and sat down heavily. Harry poured two pint-glasses of water and handed me one, then she sat down too.

'It was Dom,' I said, guzzling my water. 'He's my boyfriend. And he's married to someone else.'

'Ouch,' said Harry. 'What are you going to do about it?'

I shrugged.

'What can I do? It's his decision, isn't it?'

Harry slumped across the table dramatically.

'For heavensh shake,' she slurred. 'What do I keep telling you?'

'To shut up?' I suggested.

Harry shook her head.

'No, no, no, no,' she said. 'I keep telling you you're a witch.'

She looked serious for a minute.

'You're a really good witch, Ez,' she said. 'Use it to help you.'

She put her head on to her outstretched arm and started to snore.

'H,' I said. I shook her. There was no response. Ah well, she could stay where she was.

Chapter 24

I climbed the stairs to bed, thinking about what she'd said. Could I use witchcraft to force a resolution between me and Dom? I was wary about it, knowing what a disaster it had been when Mum cast her love spell, but I could sort of see that Harry was right. Without using magic I was doomed to sit around and wait for Dom to decide who he wanted to be with. Perhaps I could hurry him along a bit . . .

I had intended to be up with first light the next day, to read my spell book and see what I could find to help my Dom situation. As it was, I slept right through Mum and Suky going to hospital with Brent. I only woke up when Harry stuck her head round my bedroom door.

'It smells like a brewery in here,' she said cheerfully. Too cheerfully, when I considered the state she'd been in last night. 'I'm off to the café to help Eva. See you later.'

She slammed the front door so loudly the whole house shook and I forced my sorry self out of bed. Harry must have done some sort of sneaky anti-hangover spell, because I did not feel as perky as she had sounded. I made myself a bacon sandwich and a huge mug of tea, ignoring how tight my jeans were getting, then I thought about what to do about Dom.

Idly, I leafed through my spell book. Pretty much everything was covered – except how to turn a frog back into a person – and I was sure I'd find what I was looking for.

And I did. Quite near the back, in old-fashioned typeface and stuck in with yellowing Sellotape, was a charm.

'How to encourage a lover to commit,' it said. That sounded about right. If I could restore Dom's love for me, he might just decide it was time to leave Rebecca. Then we could be together and that was just what I wanted, wasn't it?

At the bottom of the sheet of paper were lots of notes written in a tiny, cramped hand. I squinted at them, but my aching head couldn't process the writing. At least the bit I needed was all typed.

Right. It was time. I put my spell book into a big canvas bag, then I sneaked into mum's 'special' cupboard at home and raided it. Into my bag I piled candles, crystals, incense and soft, white feathers. I even found a bottle of bubble mixture, so I threw that in as well along with assorted other things I thought would come in handy. All the kinds of things witches have in their store cupboards, and which, of course, I didn't have. Then I headed into town where I went to a sweet little nick-nack shop, and stocked up on tea lights and a pretty mirror with mosaic tiles round the edge.

My mind was swirling with ideas. I'd learned so much about my own abilities in the last few days and I was confident the spell would force a conclusion to my relationship with Dom. And then who knew what I could do? I thought about Brent and what he'd said about the Housewives' Guild and the rumours they were spreading. Maybe I could fend them off magically? In fact, it seemed there was no problem I couldn't solve with magic. Except for Suky's cancer, of course. Even the most powerful witch had to ask doctors for help sometimes.

I was bubbling with excitement, and oddly calm about my decision to start doing magic for myself. Maybe it wasn't magic I objected to, I thought with a flash of insight, but using it to benefit other people and not myself. Anyway, selfish or not I'd made my choice and now I couldn't wait to get started.

I hoisted my bag on to my back and headed towards the beach. I needed to go somewhere quiet, where I wouldn't be disturbed and I could get on with casting my spells in peace. I knew exactly where to go – the cave where Jamie and I had met all those years before.

Yesterday's storm had cleared and though it was still freezing cold, the air was crisp and sharp – just like it had been on the day I first found the cave. Pulling my heavy bag across my shoulder I strode across the sand and was overjoyed when I saw the boulder hiding the cave's entrance was still there. Clambering over it I dropped into the cave – it was exactly as I remembered it. Musty-smelling and dim, but cosy, dry and protected from the wind.

I settled down with my spell book, and found the page I'd marked. I scanned the spell again. It wasn't overly complicated.

I smoothed down the sand where I sat. Then I scrolled through the photos on my phone until I found a rare one of Dom and me together. Carefully I positioned it on the mirror, then scattered a box of drawing pins over the top. I arranged a circle of tea lights round the edge and lit them. The candlelight danced on the rocky walls of the cave and made the shadows twist and turn like ribbons in a breeze. It was beautiful.

Breathing deeply, I closed my eyes and re-captured the feeling I'd had at the beginning of things with Dom. That squirmy, butterfly sensation in my stomach, the thrill when I caught a glimpse of his head over the crowds on the street, and the warm rush of lust I felt when he kissed me. Then, I took a magnet and picked up all the pins. I stashed the magnet carefully in my bag. Later, I'd put it on the window ledge in my room to soak up the moonlight, but it seemed to be working already. The cave was filled with an ethereal glow that didn't come from the candles. My face was warm and my fingers tingled, despite the cold day and I felt scared and happy all at once.

On a roll now, I carried on. I lit a red candle and burned dried rose petals – picked out of a bag of pot pourri – in the flame. As the petals singed at the edges and curled up into wisps, I collected the ash in a silk hanky, and whispered: 'Commit your love to me.'

'What are you doing?'

I shrieked in surprise, burned my fingers, knocked over the candle and trod the petals into the dirt as I leapt to my feet. It was Jamie. Of course it was Jamie. No one else knew about the cave.

I whirled round to look at him. He was perched on a rock at the entrance of the cave wearing a quizzical look and a Scotland rugby shirt – just like the day we'd met. And – oh horror – above his head, the air was shimmering as the spell I'd just cast, hovered around him.

'Erm,' I gasped. 'Yoga!'

Shakily I balanced on one leg.

'I find it very relaxing.' I let out my breath in a long, wobbly wheeze and flailed at the wall of the cave, desperately trying to stay upright.

Jamie looked at me as though I was very odd.

'I saw the candlelight from the beach,' he said. 'Thought I'd come and see who'd discovered our hideout.'

I put my foot back down on the ground and clasped my hands together in what I thought might be a Zen-like pose.

'Just me,' I said, trying – and failing – to smile as I watched the shimmers softly come to a rest on the tips of Jamie's hair, the end of his nose and his broad shoulders.

'Crap,' I said softly.

Jamie raised an eyebrow.

'Sorry to disturb your workout,' he said, an amused glint in his eye. 'I'll leave you to it.'

I raised my hand to wave and he was gone; off down the beach, a trail of shimmers in his wake.

I collapsed on to the sand. Too shocked to cry, my mind raced as I thought about what I'd done.

I had cast the spell on Jamie! Flipping Jamie! After all the hoo-ha ten years ago, I'd gone and done exactly the same thing. What on earth was I going to do?

Chapter 25

At a complete loss about what to do next, I slung all my equipment into my bag and trudged back along the beach to the café.

I was horrified by what had happened but I was trying to keep my thoughts rational. Yes, I'd seen the shimmers hovering above Jamie's head, but let's be honest, I wasn't the best witch. And for a spell to be super effective, it really had to be cast by three witches – that was why I was here after all. There was a very good chance nothing had happened at all.

As I approached the café, I spotted Brent in his running gear up ahead. I went to wave, then stopped as I realised – with horror – that he was deep in conversation with Jamie. Too late, they'd seen me.

'Hi there,' Brent called. I smiled weakly.

'Hi,' I said. 'Hello, Jamie.'

Jamie gave me a half-smile that I couldn't read. Was he still annoyed with me for leaving, irritated at how strangely I'd acted earlier, or madly in love with me?

My stomach lurched as I looked at him suspiciously. There was no sign of sparkles or shimmers on the top of his hair as far as I could tell. I rose up on to my tiptoes to see better, but of course Jamie noticed.

'More yoga?'

I grimaced.

'Just stretching,' I said cheerily.

'Did you come to see me?'

Jamie looked a bit puzzled.

'Noooo,' he said cautiously. 'I'm on my lunch break and I bumped into Brent . . .'

'Great!' My fake smile got a bit wider. 'That's so great!'

Yes! He was definitely looking at me oddly. He clearly wasn't enchanted. My magic hadn't worked.

'It is nice to see you though.'

Oh. Nice? To see me? When I'd ruthlessly and unceremoniously dumped him and broken his heart? Something was definitely not right.

I stared straight into Jamie's clear blue eyes and he stared back. Then I did the only thing I could think of doing, under the circumstances.

I ran away.

Of course, I went to Chloë's. Where she took one look at my face, plonked the children in front of *Bluey* and put the kettle on. And only when we were finally sitting at her kitchen table, chocolate HobNobs open in front of us and cups of tea in our hands, did she ask what was happening.

I buried my face in my hands.

'I've done something really stupid,' I wailed. 'I've enchanted Jamie!'

Chloë grinned.

'Seriously?' She helped herself to a biscuit. 'Fabulous!'

'It is not fabulous,' I said crossly.

Chloë stuck her tongue out at me.

'I don't know what you're so worried about,' she said. 'I think you enchanted him long ago.'

I blushed.

'I didn't mean like that.'

I explained to Chloë what had happened at the beach. The spell I'd cast on Dom and which had landed on Jamie.

'So, I think the spell worked,' I said, sipping my tea. 'He said he was pleased to see me.'

Chloë chuckled.

'Get a grip, Esme,' she said. Quite sternly I thought. 'You haven't bewitched Jamie. He was pleased to see you because he likes you. A lot. It's obvious.'

I screwed up my nose. Chloë was talking nonsense. Jamie hated me. And I didn't blame him.

'And, I can't believe I have to point this out, but you like him too. There's definitely unfinished business there.'

I rolled my eyes.

'Bollocks,' I said. 'I am not in love with Jamie.'

'Ha!' shouted Chloë, triumphantly. 'I never said love. You said love! That proves it!'

I waved her away with a half-eaten HobNob.

'You don't know what you're talking about.' I was beginning to feel a bit uneasy at how the conversation was going. 'Anyway, I'm already in love. Dom is the only one for me . . .'

'Yeah, yeah, whatever,' Chloë said in glee. 'But if you're worried, why don't you go and see your mum? She'll sort out whatever magical mess you've made.'

'I don't want to.' I said.

'Go on,' she said. 'You never know, it might smooth things over a bit.'

She was right, I had to admit. Mum would know what to do. But whether or not I could bring myself to ask for her help was another matter – especially when I'd done exactly what she'd done. I did think, though, it might help me to be in the café and soak up a bit of magic. So I said goodbye and walked back towards town – I'd been back and forwards so many times today I felt dizzy.

Chapter 26

I pushed open the café door feeling sorry for myself. It was quiet with just a handful of customers. Harry was nowhere to be seen, Eva was putting her coat on and Mum was sitting on a stool by the counter, chatting to two women who I didn't recognise. I waved to her, dumped my bag on a sofa and helped myself to a cappuccino. Then I slumped down on a cushion to think.

'What's the matter?' Mum sat down next to me.

I shook my head.

'Nothing,' I said. 'Nothing you can help with, anyway.'

Mum gave me a small, sad smile.

'Why don't you try me, Esme?' she said, quite sharply. 'You never know, I might surprise you.'

I looked at her. I had nothing to lose, I supposed, and she knew a lot more about witchcraft than I did.

'I've made a massive mistake,' I said. 'I've been seeing someone – a man – at home.'

Mum looked pleased.

'Don't look like that,' I said. 'He's married.' I closed my eyes so I couldn't see her reaction. 'I thought I could cast a love spell on him – a commitment spell – and make him choose me instead of his wife.'

Mum opened her mouth to speak but I didn't let her.

'But when I did it, Mum, Jamie was there. And I cast it on him instead.'

I buried my face in my hands.

'I've done exactly what you did,' I said in despair. I may even have wailed. I certainly felt like wailing.

Mum didn't say anything. She leaned over me and picked up my bag, then she took out my spell book.

'Show me what you did,' she said. She got up and went to serve a customer, while I turned the pages miserably.

'Is this it?' she said, coming back and taking the book from me. I nodded.

With a stern face, Mum scanned the page. Then she smiled.

'You daftie,' she said. I was insulted.

'What?' I said, sulkily. 'What did I do?'

'Nothing,' she said. 'You did nothing.'

She pointed to the scribbles at the bottom of the page.

'Did you read this?'

I shook my head.

'Well, you should have,' she said. 'It's important.' She pointed to one line, which was written in capitals.

You can't bind someone to you against their will, I read.

'What does that mean?' I asked.

'It means, Esme,' Mum said, taking my hand, 'that you can't cast a love spell on someone who's not in love with you.'

'Never?'

'Never.'

'But you cast one on Jamie,' I said, bewildered.

Mum smiled at me.

'I didn't,' she said. 'I cast a spell on you, to boost your confidence. You were so unsure of yourself and I thought it might help.'

'Really?' I said, feeling guilt and shame and relief all at once.

'Really,' Mum said.

'Why didn't you tell me?' But as I spoke I remembered casting the spell that stopped me hearing Mum's voice – maybe she had told me, I wouldn't know.

'Oh Mum,' I said. 'God.'

Mum put her arm around me.

'So you didn't enchant Jamie and make him fall in love with me?' I said. 'He just actually fell in love with me.' Mum nodded. 'And I haven't enchanted him now? And I can't make Dom choose me, unless he wants to choose me?'

Mum squeezed me tight.

'No,' she said. 'You can't make someone fall in love with you. You just can't.'

I squeezed Mum back. It was the first time I'd hugged her for a really long time and it felt good.

'I'm so sorry, Mum,' I said.

She bit her lip, just like I did.

'You were right though,' she said. 'I may not have cast a love spell, but I still interfered. I should have just left you alone.'

'Yes, you should have,' I said. But suddenly it didn't hurt so much anymore.

Chapter 27

I was still thinking about going home. Suky only had a few more radiotherapy sessions left, Harry was on hand to act as a Third for Mum and Eva, and it seemed Mum and I had finally started to put our differences aside. But I was reluctant to leave immediately, just because of what was happening at the café. It was still very quiet – quieter than I'd ever seen it. Hikers and the odd hardy tourist still came in, but the regulars had turned into irregulars.

It was my turn to go with Suky to hospital and I was looking forward to having a good chat with Brent. He'd become something of a McLeod family favourite. He was driving Suky every day, and after she'd asked for help with her Wi-Fi, he often popped in later in the day to share a glass of wine with Mum. I'd seen him and Harry together the other day, heads bent over her laptop, discussing something in great detail.

Harry's business In Harmony had started online. She set it up as a safe place for witches to share ideas and tips, and it quickly grew into a forum where people could find help for their problems, or be put in touch with a practitioner (as witches were called in Harry's world). Then she started holding talks and all-day sessions, some giving training for witches, others offering self-help techniques (that's solo spell-casting to you and me)

123

for ordinary people. Now she was thinking about opening a spa and holistic therapy centre in Edinburgh and I guessed that was what she was discussing with brainy Brent. They were similar, he and Harry – both beautiful high achievers – and I thought they'd be perfect for each other if only Harry played for his team, as it were. Actually, in a way, Brent reminded me a bit of Harry's partner Natalie, who had been conspicuous by her absence since Harry arrived. It wasn't just that Nat hadn't come too, even though they'd been inseparable for years. It was more that I hadn't seen Harry call her, or heard her talk about her. It looked to me that all was not rosy in Harry and Nat's garden, but I didn't want to ask her about it.

Anyway, I was looking forward to having a good chat with Brent on the way to Inverness. I hoped he'd have more info about Millicent and the Housewives' Guild – I really wanted to know if things had got worse since my, erm, escapade with Millicent – and I wasn't disappointed.

We didn't talk about it until we were on the way home and Suky had nodded off in the back of the car.

'So, how are things at the café?' he said.

'Not great,' I said. 'Hardly anyone from the town is coming in now.'

Brent made a face that made him look a bit like Scooter from the Muppets.

'Oh hell,' he said. 'That was what I was afraid of.'

'What do you mean?'

'I think it's getting worse,' he said. 'I called round to Millicent's the other day to have a look through her accounts.'

'You're becoming indispensable to everyone in town,' I said. The thought irked me, though I couldn't really say why.

'Anyway, she was asking me about you guys and how much I was seeing you. I said I drove you to Suky's appointments and she was kind of funny about it.'

'Funny how?' I said, feeling my stomach drop into my Uggs.

'Just asking me if I knew what kind of people you were and saying I should think about my involvement with you.'

'God,' I said. 'That's not great.'

'And I've heard other people say similar stuff,' Brent said. He changed gear and accelerated away from a junction.

'At first it was sort of jokey, you know. They were saying Suky was magic,' he chuckled. 'But now – it's crazy, but I've heard people say you're witches.'

I looked out of the window so he wouldn't see my face.

'That is crazy,' I said. 'Thank goodness no one will listen to them.'

'I wouldn't be so sure,' Brent said. He paused while he went round a roundabout, then carried on. 'Mud sticks, Ez. Just be careful, OK?'

Chapter 28

I'd planned to do some work that afternoon. I'd not so much as checked in with Maggie for days and I hadn't a clue what was happening with any of my cases, but I just couldn't settle. My mind was racing with worries about what the people in the town were saying about us, not to mention thoughts of Dom who'd not been texting or phoning as much as I'd have liked him to. Plus I kept seeing Jamie around. He was polite but distant and made it quite clear he didn't want to be my friend. So much for Chloë's unfinished business. Now I knew Mum hadn't cast a love spell, I felt like I should apologise to him but I had no idea how to bring it up without telling him the whole truth. And with the way Claddach was treating us at the moment, I thought telling more people about the McLeod family's special skills was most definitely not the right thing to do.

So eventually, I switched off my laptop and headed out for a walk, hoping it would clear my head a bit. It was wild outside – lashing rain and wind that made putting up an umbrella nearly impossible.

I stomped down the hill towards town with the wind whipping my hair across my face and making me wince. Irritated, I yanked my tangled locks back and twisted them into a knot, securing it with a biro I found at the bottom of my bag and carried on.

Narrowing my eyes against the blustery wind, I marched through town not really sure where I was heading. As I passed the Post Office, I glanced at my reflection in the window and stopped, appalled at what I saw.

I was hunched down in my enormous padded jacket and my hair was a tangled lump perched on the back of my head, with a broken Bic emerging from the top. My jeans were dirty and – I leaned forward to look more closely – I'd apparently only put mascara on one eye that morning.

I grimaced at myself in the window, then moved away quickly as old Mrs Adams, inside in the queue to collect her pension, grimaced back in confusion. Something had to be done about my appearance and quickly – I'd not been home long but already the stylish career woman I'd once been had disappeared. Checking my watch – I had time before I had to take over at the café – I ducked into the tiny local branch of Boots. It was time for an emergency new lipstick.

'Settlin' in all right, are you?'

Surprised, I looked up from the tube of Natural Blush I was testing on my hand. The woman who worked in the shop was looking at me. I didn't know her, she'd moved to Claddach after I'd left, but she obviously knew me. She was leaning over her counter, chatting with an older woman who was wearing a hat like a tea cosy.

I smiled carefully, not really understanding what was happening.

'It's been a while,' I said, tucking the lipstick into my palm, and picking up one in bright red, which was much more Harry's colour than mine.

'Do you need any help?' the assistant asked. She had long stringy hair and was younger that I'd first thought – probably in her late 30s. She could do with getting a new lipstick herself, I thought unkindly, looking at her pale, bare face. I shook my head.

'I know what I'm after, thanks,' I said, turning my attention to the nail varnishes.

'I'm not sure I've got anything for you,' the woman said pointedly.

Her tea-cosy-headed friend giggled girlishly, making my heart lurch with nerves. What did she mean by that? I looked at her suspiciously.

'I like make-up,' I said firmly. Ignoring the butterflies that were flapping their wings frantically in my stomach, I turned away from both women slightly. I pretended to be engrossed in the nail varnishes, but actually I was straining to hear what they were saying. She didn't mean anything by that, I told myself. She didn't know anything about us. How could she?

I glanced at the women over the top of the blushers. They were both leaning on the counter, their heads close together. Stringy Hair was speaking softly and Tea Cosy was listening, her eyes widening in astonishment.

I edged slightly closer.

'So many strange goings on,' I heard her mutter. 'Pam from the new estate says she's never been right since she ate that scone.'

I relaxed, reaching into my bag for my purse. The miserable cow obviously didn't like Mum's cooking. Juggling the two lipsticks in my hand, I scrabbled around the bottom of my cavernous sack, only half-listening to their conversation.

'We should have a meeting,' Tea Cosy was saying. Stringy Hair nodded. 'Something needs to be done,' she agreed. 'I've already spoken to Millicent.'

That got my attention. Why on earth had she been speaking to Mrs Fry? My hands shook, and desperate to shut the gossiping women up, I dropped my purse on to the tiled floor with a thud. The women jumped guiltily.

'Sorry,' I sang gaily, with a forced confidence I didn't really feel.

'Everything OK?' Tea Cosy looked at me, her small eyes narrow in her pale face. I felt she was challenging me. I looked back, unsmiling.

'Great hat,' I said. She scowled at me.

'I'll give you a ring later,' she said to Stringy Hair and scuttled out of the door.

'£15,' Stringy Hair said to me, holding out her hand. Her nails were bitten right down her fingers and she had hard skin on her palms. I felt a flicker of sympathy for her.

'You work at that café,' she said accusingly, her lips set in a tight line. 'It's not right.'

'What isn't right?' All my sympathy disappeared. 'Do you not like the cakes?' I tapped my card on the machine.

Stringy Hair opened the till with a sharp prod at the keys and paused, considering what to say next.

'We don't want the likes of you here,' she said, handing me my receipt and stuffing her copy in the till. 'Everyone agrees with me. We've decided we're not going to sit back and let you carry on with this, this – 'she waved her hand in the air as if conjuring up the right word '– this monkey business.' She finished with a triumphant nod.

My heart plummeted again. If the Housewives' Guild were already drumming up allies for some sort of campaign against us, then things were worse than I'd thought, but I wasn't about to let old Stringy Hair see she had me rattled.

'I don't know what you mean,' I said cheerfully, gathering up my lipsticks and heading for the door. 'Give my best to Pam from the new estate, won't you? And do pop into the café for a flapjack sometime.'

Fixing a grin on my face, I shut the shop door behind me with a bang and went to find my mum.

I was in luck. She and Harry were both in the café. Harry was bent over her laptop again, and Mum was standing behind the counter, lost in thought. She didn't even look up as I approached.

'Mum,' I said. She jumped.

'Oh hello, Ez,' she said.

'Mum, I need to tell you something,' I said. 'Come and sit down.' She looked at me vaguely.

'Ez, have you noticed how quiet it's been in here?'

I sat down next to Harry, who looked annoyed at the inter-ruption, and kicked the chair out from opposite so mum could sit down too.

'That's what I wanted to talk to you about,' I said. 'I think there's a problem.'

Quickly, I told her what Suky had told me about the spells going wrong, then I filled her in on the information Brent had passed on.

'And you think this Millicent is gossiping about us?' Mum said, resting her chin on her hands.

'I do,' I said. 'Suky turned her into an insatiable sex addict. She must have been so embarrassed.'

Harry looked up. 'Tell her what you did,' she said.

'I don't think that's relevant,' I said.

Harry tapped her keyboard a few times, then closed the laptop.

'Esme turned her into a frog,' she said cheerfully. 'I shouldn't think that helped much.'

Mum looked surprised and impressed all at once.

'You said she wouldn't remember,' I hissed at Harry. She shrugged.

'Probably won't,' she said. 'But there's always a chance.'

I glared at her and she stopped talking.

'It does seem odd,' Mum said. 'But even if this Millicent has taken against us, then what can she do, really? She's just one woman.'

'But I was just in the chemist,' I said. 'The women in there were horrible. They said they didn't want us in town.'

'Ah,' said Mum. 'I see. But even so, it's just gossip.'

'So it's not just Millicent and it's not just gossip.' I was getting frustrated. 'If she persuades the village that we're something to be afraid of, she could shut us down.'

'I don't think . . .'

'She could!' I interrupted. 'People are so suspicious nowadays – Eva told me that someone on the village WhatsApp group shared a photo of a chap loitering outside the big houses. They were warning everyone to be aware because he could have been casing the joint, and it turned out to be the postman. They just couldn't see his uniform because it was misty.'

'I think you're catastrophising, Esme,' Mum laughed and I scowled back. 'I do think it sounds a bit strange but as long as we keep an eye on things, we'll be fine.'

I wasn't convinced though, and I was pretty sure Mum wasn't either – despite her bold talk.

'Thank goodness we've got Brent,' I said as Mum got up to serve a customer. 'It's so useful that all the women in the Housewives' Guild adore him – he's like our mole.'

Harry scrunched her face up.

'I'm not sure about him,' she said. 'I can't get a handle on him.'

I was offended on Brent's behalf.

'I thought you liked him?'

'I do,' Harry said. 'At least, I like the bit of him he shows.'

'What do you mean?'

'He's just so perfect, you know? Helping me with my business plan for the spa, helping your mum with her internet, driving Suky to hospital, making sure we're warned about the gossip.'

'You're so cynical,' I said in disgust. 'Sometimes people are just really nice.'

'I can't read his aura,' she said. 'That always makes me suspicious.'

I snorted at her.

'He's just a nice person,' I said. 'You're probably not used to meeting them.'

She looked at me with narrowed eyes.

'Fine,' she said. 'Don't believe me. But I think we should find another way to infiltrate the group – just in case.'

I quite liked that.

'Like a double agent?' I said.

Harry looked round to make sure no one was listening.

Unlikely as there were only about five customers in the café. Then she pulled her chair closer to mine.

'A spy to spy on our spy,' she said.

That made me uncomfortable. Brent had been very good to us and I didn't want her upsetting him.

'More a spy to back up the intelligence provided by our original spy,' I said.

Harry shrugged.

'Whatever,' she said. 'But we need to get the right person. Who should we ask?'

We both thought for a moment.

'Ooh, I know,' I said. 'What about Nell?'

Harry looked blank.

'She's one of Eva's latest lambs,' I said. 'She loves your mum and she hates Millicent. She'll do it.'

'Excellent,' Harry said. 'You sort that out then.'

She started gathering her papers together.

'And Ez? Please don't mention this to Mum. She's not doing so well.'

Chapter 29

Poor Suky really wasn't doing so well. The radiotherapy was really taking its toll. She had swelling across her chest and her torso was red, tender and sore. She was so tired that she spent every afternoon sleeping, but then couldn't sleep at night. She'd lost her appetite so she was getting thinner and thinner, despite Mum's efforts to tempt her with a succession of delicious meals. But worse than all that was the way she was in herself. It was like she'd simply given up. She lay on the sofa, glassy-eyed. She didn't want to read books or watch TV. She refused to talk about anything in the future. Mum mentioned Christmas one day and Suky's eyes flashed with anger. When I went with her to hospital, she sat in the back seat of Brent's Range Rover and looked out of the window, or slept. She never spoke to us now. In fact, the only person who really talked to her was Harry. She would go into her mum's room most evenings, with her iPad and a large black canvas bag that I knew she kept in her room, and not come out until Suky had, eventually, dropped off to sleep. More than once, on my way to bed, I'd noticed magic hanging around the hallway, or sparks lighting up the space under the bedroom door. It was strange magic though. You know how fire is always orange – always – unless it's the fire on your gas hob, when it's a blue flame? It was kind of like that. It looked like magic, but it was different. I didn't know enough about magic to know why. Was it Suky's illness making things change? Or was it a different kind of magic altogether?

'What are you doing in there?' I asked Harry one evening. 'Is Suky doing magic?'

'Magic?' Harry had said, as if it was the most ridiculous thing she'd ever heard. 'No. No magic.'

But I didn't believe her. I thought about Suky telling me Harry had been researching different cures for her cancer and wondered if they were cooking up something between themselves.

So of course I agreed when Harry asked me not to mention the goings on at the café to Suky. I really didn't want to make things worse.

Instead, I tracked down Nell at Eva's studio. She was wrapping some of Eva's gigantic fruit bowls in bubble wrap and putting them gently into boxes to be taken to shops all over Scotland.

'Wow,' I said, picking one up. It was huge – about half a metre across – and shallow, with a delicate design that echoed the colours of the mountains and the sea.

'They're amazing, aren't they?' Nell said. 'Eva's teaching me how to throw like her.'

'Can I help you?' I said. 'You wrap and I'll put them in the boxes.'

'OK,' she said. Together we worked in silence for a while.

'Nell,' I said eventually. 'We need your help.'

She looked dubious.

'Doing what?'

I explained that we thought the Housewives' Guild were gossiping about us and damaging business.

'Would you go to some meetings?' I asked. 'Maybe see if that Imogen can tell you anything.'

Nell sat down on the bench the bowls had been stacked on.

'I don't know,' she said. She pushed the sleeve of her jumper up to her elbow and held her arm out to me. Across her smooth skin were the silvery cobwebs of her scars.

'I did this,' she said. She sounded defiant and a bit scared. 'When things were really bad at school. I did it to myself.'

I didn't know what to say.

'Eva's helped me a lot,' she said. 'And Suky. Imogen wasn't at our school then, but she's friends with those girls. I just can't help wondering if she'll make me go back to all that.'

'Don't do it,' I said, feeling guilty for asking. 'I'm sorry, I didn't realise.'

But Nell lifted her chin.

'No,' she said. 'I'll do it. I'm stronger now and I want to repay Eva and Suky for how kind they've been.'

'Are you sure?'

'I'm sure,' she said. 'But they know I work at the café – they won't want me in their meetings.'

In the end, we came up with a plan. Imogen, weirdly, was one of the café's few regulars who had kept coming.

'No one tells her what to do,' Nell had pointed out. 'Not even her mum.'

The next day, when Imogen came in after school and sat at her usual table, alone, I texted Nell.

Ten minutes later, she arrived, face flushed and with an armful of books – she'd obviously come straight from school herself.

'I'm so sorry!' she wailed as she came through the door. The few customers who were in the café stopped chatting and looked up. Imogen narrowed her eyes.

'Mum says I can't work here anymore,' Nell hiccupped. 'She doesn't want me mixing with you people.'

I gasped, more at Nell's Oscar-worthy performance than what she was saying, then I reached out my hand and rubbed Nell's arm.

'But Nell,' I said. 'We love working with you.'

Nell cried louder, shrugging off my hand and burying her face in her scarf. I wondered for a moment if she was going too far.

Then I caught her eye as she hid under her woolly refuge and she winked. Good girl. I opened the till and took out a £20 note.

'I'm sorry you feel that way,' I said in a cold voice. 'I think this covers what we owe you.' I handed her the money. 'Close the door on your way out.'

Nell spun round and marched out of the café. Imogen waited a moment, then she got up and scuttled out after her. Job done.

The rest of my shift was uneventful. It was quiet as usual, and I even managed time to go through my work emails and call Maggie.

'Suky's got one more week of treatment,' I said. 'I'd like to stay until it's finished if that's OK?'

'Do whatever you have to do,' said Maggie. There were some advantages to never having had a day off until now.

With that weight lifted, I'd shut up my laptop, put my phone away, and gone back to worrying about what to do if the people in Claddach turned against us.

Just before closing time, as I was writing down some PR ideas (well, they were more like bribes, really) – free coffee at weekends, free Wi-Fi, free cakes with every cup of tea, free cakes generally – Jamie came in.

He gave me the half-smile I was getting used to.

'Latte please,' he said. 'To go.'

I made the coffee, knowing I had to apologise for what had happened all those years ago.

'On the house,' I said, handing him the cup.

'Oh no,' he said. 'You don't have to do that . . .'

'Just take the damn coffee,' I snapped. Jamie looked alarmed.

'Sorry,' I said. 'Listen, can we sit down for a minute.'

Jamie checked his watch.

'I've got five minutes,' he said. 'What's up?'

'I just wanted to tell you something,' I said. 'When I left, you know, back then . . .'

Jamie's expression changed from mildly interested to stony.

'It doesn't matter,' he said. 'It was a long time ago. It's over. I just never understood what I did wrong. One minute you were there, the next you were gone.'

'You didn't do anything, Jamie. It was all me.'

He gave me a wry smile that had absolutely no humour in it.

'It's not you, it's me?'

'Yes,' I said. 'But not like that.'

The conversation was not going at all how I wanted it to go.

'I can't explain,' I said. 'I just knew it was the right thing to do.'

'For you, perhaps,' he said. 'I was a mess when you left.'

I felt guilty all over again.

'I had to go away,' I said.

'You could have given me some warning. I didn't even have time to get used to the idea.' Jamie ran his fingers through his hair and made it stick up.

'I thought you would have wanted to change my mind about leaving,' I said, knowing it was no excuse at all for going without saying goodbye.

'So you didn't even give me a chance to try? That wasn't fair, Esme.'

'I meant to,' I said softly. 'The whole time I was planning to leave, I meant to tell you. But when the time came I just couldn't face you.'

'Coward,' said Jamie. The ice in his voice made me wince.

'I didn't want to make things harder. It was much easier to go.' I rubbed my nose.

'I want to explain,' I said, talking quickly so he couldn't interrupt. 'It's just I thought Mum had done something that made you want to be with me, so I had to go because I was cross and embarrassed, and I thought you should find yourself a girlfriend that you really wanted to be with . . .'

I trailed off as I realised he was staring at me in confusion.

'You thought your mum had done something?' he repeated. 'Like what?'

I was at a loss. I couldn't tell him I'd thought it was a love spell.

'Like a bribe?' he carried on. 'Did you think she'd paid me?'

'Yes!' I said. 'Exactly that. I thought she'd paid you to go out with me.'

Jamie shook his head.

'Bloody hell, Ez,' he said. 'Is that what you think of me?'

Then he chuckled.

'Is that what you think of yourself? That your mum has to pay men to go out with you?'

I scratched at a bump on the table.

'Well, not now,' I said defensively. 'Now I get my own boyfriends.'

'Good for you,' he said. He gave me a strange look. 'So you've got a boyfriend, have you?'

'I have actually.' I said. But as I was saying it, I realised I didn't want him to know about Dom. Not if it made him think less of me – as if that was even possible – and not if it made him think I was off the market. Stupid Esme, talking first without thinking of the consequences.

'Good for you,' he said again. 'I've got to go.' He stood up. 'Thanks for explaining,' he said awkwardly. 'I'll see you around.'

As he left, I felt deflated. My apology had gone as well as I could have hoped. I wasn't sure what I'd expected. Did I want Jamie to fall into my arms and say he still loved me? No. After all, I didn't have any feelings for him. Or did I? I thought about how his eyes crinkled at the edges when he smiled and his slightly crooked teeth, and his broad shoulders and narrow waist. I thought about how he'd kissed me all those years ago and told me we were meant to be together. I thought about Chloë saying we had unfinished business and suddenly I realised she was right. Seeing Jamie again had stirred up feelings I thought had been buried long ago and I had no idea what to do about them.

Chapter 30

I closed up the café, it took no time at all now I used witchcraft instead of elbow grease, and walked up the hill towards home. The weather was getting worse every day. Halloween was just around the corner, and autumn was on its way out – winter was definitely knocking on Claddach's door. Wet leaves whipped round my ankles and though it wasn't raining, there was a chilly dampness in the air that left my hair frizzy and my nose red.

When I got home, Harry was sitting at the kitchen table. She had spread paperwork out in front of her but she wasn't reading it; instead she had her head in her hands. Her hair was loose around her shoulders and she was wearing jeans and a soft grey jumper. She looked human for once – and very upset. I took a step towards her.

'Harry?' I said, putting a hand on her shoulder (ooh, cashmere. Nice).

'Is everything OK?'

Harry jumped and started shuffling papers together.

'I was just catching up on paperwork.' She grabbed a letter that was on top of a pile and started folding it up, but she wasn't quick enough to stop me spotting a law firm's headed notepaper. I snatched it from her manicured hand.

'What's this?' I said.

Harry hesitated for a moment, then gave in. She sunk into her chair and her eyes filled with tears.

'I'm being sued,' she admitted. 'I'm scared it's going to ruin my reputation and all my plans for the spa. What if I lose everything?'

I leaned over her shoulder and scanned the letter. It was threatening, I had to admit, and if I'd been Harry I'd have been terrified. But to a finely-honed legal brain like mine (or, in fact, to anyone who had so much as law A-level) it was less scary.

'So this client came to you for aura cleansing,' I said. Harry nodded woefully.

'But she says since then she's had terrible bad luck and that means her aura is . . .' I swallowed a giggle, Harry didn't take kindly to people mocking her profession.

'It means her aura is dirty.'

Harry nodded again.

'She's suing for loss of earnings, for medical bills, nutrition advice – even a new haircut,' she said. 'It could be thousands of pounds. But it's the damage to my reputation that will be worse. I can never get that back.' She ran her fingers through her hair in despair and I felt sorry for her. This was the last thing she needed when Suky was so ill.

'I can help,' I said, hoping I wouldn't regret it. 'I'll tell you a secret about lawyers. We'll write a scary letter to pretty much anyone about pretty much anything, if we're being paid. This letter means nothing.'

Harry looked slightly less frightened.

'I'll write an equally threatening response,' I continued. 'And I reckon that's the last you'll hear about it all.'

Harry relaxed noticeably. She leaned her head back so it was resting on my tummy as I stood behind her. It was such an intimate gesture that I felt immediately awkward. Stiffly I patted her head.

'It'll be OK,' I said. 'In fact, I'm going to do it now, while I'm in the mood.'

Filled with warmth for doing such a good deed, I booted up my laptop once more. Then I drafted a threatening-yet-meaningless legal letter and presented it triumphantly to Harry, who was thrilled.

'You have a knack for this stuff,' she said in surprise. 'Who knew?'

'I knew,' I said, crossly. 'And all my clients. Thank you very much.'

'So you reckon I'll send this and she'll back off,' she said.

'I do,' I said. 'She's just trying her luck.'

Harry relaxed back into the chair.

'Was that the problem at work?' I asked.

'One of them,' she said. 'It's just all a bit much on my own, you know.'

'Is Natalie not helping?'

'She's gone back to the States,' Harry said, her lips so pursed I could hardly see them. 'I'm not sure when she'll be back.'

There was a pause. 'I'm not sure she's going to come back at all, actually.'

I was shocked.

'What's happened?'

Harry smiled ruefully.

'Oh we've grown apart, we met too young, blah blah blah,' she said. 'She wanted to go back to the States and I wanted to stay here. Pick your reason.'

I put my arm round her.

'Sorry, H,' I said. 'Things will get better soon.'

'Yeah well they'd better,' she said. She turned to look at me. 'Enough about my sorry old love life. What about yours?'

'Nothing to report,' I said, thinking about Jamie. 'Nothing at all.'

'What about your married man?'

'Oh him.' I hadn't even considered she'd mean Dom. That wasn't a good sign. 'Nothing to report.'

'So you haven't done anything about it?'

'Nope.'

'Shall we do it?' Her face lit up.

'Nope,' I said again.

Harry's shoulders slumped.

'Aw Ez, go on. Let's do something.'

I was tempted, I couldn't deny it. I really didn't want to go back to London without having some sort of resolution to my relationship with Dom.

'Oh go on then,' I said. 'What shall we do?'

'We need to know what he's really thinking,' Harry said. 'That's easy to do when someone's here – unless they're Brent of course.' Her inability to read Brent was really bothering her.

'Oh get over it, H,' I said. 'What do we do if someone isn't here?'

She thought for a moment, brows furrowed. Then her face cleared.

'Is he on Skype or Zoom or whatever?'

I nodded.

'We all are – we often use it for video conferences.'

'Let's try that,' she said. 'Ring him and tell him you want to see him.'

'Then what?'

'We'll get him on Skype and I'll do my thing.'

'Do you think it'll work?'

'It's worth a try,' she said. 'You want to know, don't you?'

I nodded slowly. I did want to know. Was there any future in my relationship with Dom or not?

I picked up my phone and scrolled to his number. Hopefully he would be working late and able to talk.

He answered straight away and I put him on speakerphone.

'I was just about to call you,' he said. He sounded flustered. 'I miss you.'

I melted. Harry frowned at me and pointed to the laptop.

'I miss you too,' I said. 'Can we Skype?'

'Brilliant plan,' said Dom. 'Can we do it naked?'

Harry made a mock shocked expression.

'My cousin is here with me,' I said primly. 'I thought you might want to meet her.'

'The evil one?'

Swiftly I took the phone off speaker as Harry glowered at me.

'Nooo, not that one,' I said. 'A completely different cousin. I'm going to Skype you now.'

I hung up, not wanting to look at Harry but she laughed.

'He'd better do what I want him to do,' she said, as I connected to Skype. 'Or he'll see how evil I can really be.'

It was strange to see Dom sitting at his desk. I introduced him to Harry and saw his womaniser radar light up when he clocked how gorgeous she was.

'It is really nice to meet you, Harry,' he said smoothly.

'Oh for God's sake, put your tongue away,' I snapped at him.

'Woah, Ez,' he said. 'I was just being polite.' He held up his hand as if to hold me back and the light glinted off his wedding ring.

Dom filled me in on a bit of work stuff, and I glanced at Harry. She was sitting very still, eyes half closed, and the air around her was shimmering.

'So, Dom,' she said, interrupting him as he told me something about Maggie. 'Tell me about your wife.'

The air around the kitchen table shimmered and – I leant towards the laptop screen, just to check I wasn't imagining it – the air around Dom was shimmering too. Harry was so good at this.

'Rebecca's great,' Dom sighed. 'She's beautiful and funny and she knows me inside out. We've been together since we were eighteen.'

I shifted uncomfortably in my seat. I did not want to hear this. Through the screen, Harry stared right into Dom's eyes. He stared back, transfixed.

'And what are you doing with my Esme?' she asked.

Dom breathed in deeply.

'Rebecca's just – you know?'

'What?' I said harshly. 'What is she?'

143

'She's too grown up,' Dom admitted. 'She wants to have a baby.' The word hung over the table and lodged in a dark part of my heart. I stared at him. Planning a baby was not a usual conversation for a couple who were on the brink of a divorce.

'A baby?' I repeated.

'Makes sense,' said Harry lightly. 'You've been together for years. It's the next step.'

'I'm too young to be tied down.' Dom looked at Harry for approval. 'I'm only thirty-five.'

Harry nodded.

'You want to sow some wild oats, hedge your bets . . .'

Dom smiled, obviously relieved that Harry understood. I was not happy.

'Esme's a bit of fun,' he said, looking into the distance and obviously remembering how much fun we'd had. I blushed but Harry wasn't paying any attention to me.

'Rebecca's the same age as me, and it's different for women, isn't it?' Dom said. 'Her clock's ticking.'

Harry –who was a year older – narrowed her eyes at him.

'I think we've heard enough,' she said, looking at me.

Dom rubbed his eyes, as though he'd just woken up. Which, in a way, he had.

'What was I saying?' he said. 'I've lost my train of thought.'

I was feeling prickly. I was cross with Dom for revealing himself to be such an idiot, cross with Harry for making him admit it and grudgingly grateful that she had.

'You were just talking about Rebecca,' I said, forcing a smile at him, even though I didn't feel like it.

Dom looked alarmed.

'Was I?' he said. 'God.'

Quietly Harry got up and left the kitchen, leaving me alone. I knew what I had to do.

'Are you going to leave her?' Dom looked down at his desk, then back at me. There was a light in his eyes that I couldn't interpret.

'I don't know,' he said. Suddenly he looked very young and a little bit scared. 'I thought I knew what I wanted, but I don't.'

'What's happening, Dom?'

'I love you,' he said simply. 'But I love Rebecca, too. I think she knows about us.'

I was horrified.

'Does she? But we've been so careful.'

'Well, she knows I've been up to something. I've got form, Esme. This isn't the first time I've cheated on her.'

'It's not?'

Dom laughed without humour.

'No, it's not. But last time she said if I did it again I'd be out.'

I stared at him through the screen. Seeing him for what he really was.

'Are you cheating on me?' I said, knowing the answer.

'No,' he said. But some of Harry's truth spell must have lingered because then he looked down. 'Well, Vicky and I . . . you know, we were drunk, it was late . . .'

'You horrible man,' I said. 'You horrible, mean, shitty man.'

Dom did manage to look slightly sorry.

'Are you going to leave Rebecca?' I asked.

Dom looked straight into my eyes, through the screen.

'No,' he said. 'No, I'm not.'

My stomach lurched and I thought I was going to be sick. But almost immediately I realised that hearing the words I'd dreaded for so long wasn't as bad as I thought it would be.

'Then you need to fight for her,' I said. 'Make her see that you're there for her. That there's no one else. And you need to make sure that there is no one else. Not me, not Vicky, not anyone.'

I felt very close to tears, but I didn't want Dom to see me cry.

Dom nodded.

'I'm sorry,' he whispered.

'No you're not,' I said. 'Not really.'

Dom shrugged.

'I'll see you around,' he said, reaching over to turn off his computer.

'See you around,' I said.

I closed the laptop, then I put my head in my hands and cried.

Chapter 31

At some point, Harry came back into the room. She put her arms round me and I wept on her shoulder while she stroked my hair and muttered meaningless words of comfort into my ear.

Then she phoned Chloë, who came up the hill with two bottles of wine and a supersized bar of Dairy Milk like an avenging angel and she and Harry sat patiently and listened – and drank the wine – as I wailed and wept and cursed myself for wasting so long on Dom.

I spent the whole of the next day in bed, only emerging to make cups of tea before heading back to my room. I didn't want to see anyone. I was heartbroken, and angry, and embarrassed and I needed time to myself to get things straight in my head.

I would have stayed in bed the next day, too, but Harry came into my room and opened the curtains.

'Up,' she said. 'We need you.'

I turned over to face the wall and pulled the duvet tighter round my shoulders.

Harry yanked it off the bed completely, leaving me exposed to the elements.

'Harry,' I whined. 'I'm not up to it. Give me the duvet back.'

'No,' Harry said. 'My mum needs someone to go to hospital

with her, Nell's been to her first meeting and wants to tell us about it, and I have to open up at the café.'

Furious at not being allowed to wallow in my despair, I dragged myself into the shower and threw on some clothes. Then I went downstairs to talk Harry into letting me open up at the café instead.

'I'm just not up to making small talk with Brent,' I said.

But Harry wouldn't budge.

'I've got stuff to do,' she said. 'I need it done by the end of the week.'

'What's the end of the week?' I asked. Harry shrugged but she didn't elaborate. It was Halloween at the end of the week. I wondered if it had anything to do with the strange magic I'd seen in Suky's room, but I didn't much care. I didn't really care about anything except Dom.

When Brent pulled up outside, I listlessly helped Suky into his car, then I climbed in as well.

'Are you OK?' he asked as we drove off.

'Fine,' I said shortly. I didn't want to explain.

'I don't blame you for being worried about the café,' he said. 'It's your family's livelihood and it's at risk.'

I looked at him wearily.

'What?' I said. 'What are you saying?'

'The café,' he repeated. 'It's at risk.'

It was what I'd been worried about all along, but to hear someone else voice my concerns gave me a jolt. I sat up.

'Do you think so?' I said.

'I know so,' Brent changed gear and swung round a corner on to the main road out of town.

'I know a bit about business and I know how much is built on reputation,' he said. I remembered Harry's fears about the threats made against her business and thought he was probably right. 'In a town like this, you'll be fine in the summer – there will always be the tourist trade. But that's not going to sustain a business through the winter. For that you need a good reputation.'

'Do you think we're losing that reputation?'

'Definitely,' he said. 'The gossip those women are spreading is ridiculous but if it's stopping people coming to the café then you're in trouble. And,' he paused.

'What?'

'From what I've heard it's getting more personal,' he said. 'People are beginning to think you and your family are sinister. Satanists. Weirdos, anyway. They don't want you living near them.'

'Well that's just silly,' I said. 'It's not like they can do anything to make us leave. What are they going to do? Run us out of town? Just for being a bit different?'

'It happens,' Brent said darkly. I thought he was being a bit overdramatic.

'It's just gossip,' I said. 'Sticks and stones . . .'

Brent looked at me uncomprehendingly.

'Oh never mind,' I said, glancing into the back seat where Suky sat silently, staring out of the window as always. 'I'll worry if they come up with a concrete plan to get rid of us. Until then, I'm going to concentrate on Suky.'

We pulled up in our usual spot and I helped Suky out of the car. She was so sore now – her treatment had left her chest battered and raw – that walking was difficult.

She hung on to my arm as we walked to the oncology department and I felt so sorry for her. She was a shadow of her normal self – I just hoped she'd get her spark back when this was all over.

It was the beginning of her third and final week of radiotherapy.

'Knowing it's nearly over is all that's keeping me going,' she told me as she put on the hospital gown. 'This time next week, it's finished.'

I did up the ties at her back.

'You're doing so well,' I said, knowing it sounded terribly patronising. 'Just a few more days.'

Once again, Suky fell asleep almost as soon as we got into Brent's car. I'd decided to sit in the back with her, so I held her

149

hand all the way home and thought about what Brent had said. I still thought he was being a prophet of doom. I just couldn't see how a few women, led by an Englishwoman in a tartan hat, could get the better of us.

But I'd underestimated the Housewives' Guild.

We got home and I bustled Suky into bed.

'I'm so bored,' she complained.

'I know,' I said, as I tucked her in like a child. 'Maybe later you could go for a walk if you feel up to it?'

'Whoopee,' she said.

I left her to sleep and went downstairs to do a bit of work. Then I went for a run along the shores of the loch and when I came home Suky was gone. I smiled to myself, thinking she'd gone for that walk after all, and decided to go down to the café to see what was going on. Weirdly, Brent being so bleak about it all had made me feel a bit better. I just couldn't see that it was as bad as he was making out.

Bit when I turned to go down the path towards the café I stopped in shock, all my fears coming true at once. The Housewives' Guild most definitely had a plan – and it was happening right in front of me.

Chapter 32

I blinked in disbelief. Outside the café was a group of perhaps twenty or thirty women, wrapped up in cagoules and wellies, and shouting. Loudly.

I took a step closer, willing them to be a figment of my imagination. But no, they were real all right. I picked out Stringy Hair, and scanned the crowd for Millicent. She was there, standing at the very edge. I imagined she'd spread the word to get the women riled up and was now standing back and watching her poison work.

'Our village, our homes and our families are at stake,' one woman was saying. 'Are we going to stand by and watch while these tricksters take our money and undermine our values?'

I gasped as the women cheered in agreement. It was a bit like being at a Harry Styles concert only the screaming tweenage girls had been replaced by screaming middle-aged women.

Another woman spoke up.

'We're all generous, thoughtful, welcoming women,' she said, her words carrying over the wind. 'But even we have limits. This café is a risk to our moral, emotional and spiritual health and we won't stand for it!'

The women whooped.

Whooped.

Slightly nervous for my own safety, I slunk into the shadows, trying to think of a way to get into the café without being seen.

'We want this café shut down! And we want its owners gone!' another woman shouted.

The women were whipping themselves into a frenzy. They were waving placards – placards for heaven's sake – which said CLAW! I had no idea what it meant, but I knew it wasn't good.

Zipping up my jacket I twisted my hair into a knot and tucked it into my hood. Then I fished in my bag, found my sunglasses – it was drizzling and overcast but never mind – and stuck them on too. As disguises went, it wasn't brilliant but it would have to do. I was hoping the women were so wrapped up in their literal witch hunt that they would ignore me.

Staring straight ahead, I walked confidently past the women. None of them saw me. Cosy in their North Face fleeces and fluffy ear muffs, they were bouncing up and down, waving their placards, and shouting: 'Claddach Ladies Against Witches!'

Ah. CLAW. Now I understood their slogan. Keeping my head down I hurried to the door of the café, but just as I put my hand on the knob, the shouting stopped. I froze.

'There she is!' Stringy Hair called over the heads of the CLAWs. 'Take a good look at that face! She's not welcome in our village.'

In shock I stared at the hostile faces of the women that surrounded me. Their eyes were wide, their teeth bared in primal aggression. I stood up straighter, and, for a moment, I considered taking them on. But the moment passed as quickly as it had arrived and instead I pushed myself through the door, slammed it behind me and bolted it tight shut.

Breathing deeply I leaned against the doorframe and gazed in bewilderment at the empty café.

'What is going on?' I gasped.

Out of nowhere, Mum appeared, grasped my hand and pulled me into the kitchen. Suky and Eva were sitting round the table looking worried. I hugged them all, being especially gentle with Suky because I knew how sore she was.

'What are you doing here?' I asked her. 'I told you to go for a walk, but I didn't mean for you to come all the way down here.'

'I just felt like getting out of the house.' She gave me a weak smile. 'And look what happened.'

'Where's Harry?' I said, looking round. 'Does she know what's going on?'

'I've left her a message,' Mum said. 'But she's not rung back yet.'

'She's doing some work,' Suky said, a little defensively. 'She said she'd be down later . . .'

Harry hadn't been at home when I was. I thought about mentioning it, but changed my mind as the noise outside increased.

Suddenly I was furious. What were we doing, hiding out in the kitchen like criminals? I pushed open the kitchen door and looked out of the café's long windows. The women were still there, their shouts carried away on the wind.

Angrily, I stomped out into the café and peering through the window I did a quick headcount. There were twenty people outside. Right.

Working quickly, I made twenty lattes, then I dumped twenty cupcakes on to plates and laid them all on trays. Mum, Suky and Eva had come out of the kitchen and were watching me in silence. I beckoned to them.

'Come on,' I said, waving my arm over the trays. 'Let's try something. Anything.'

Mum shook her head.

'No magic, Ez,' she said quietly. 'Not now.'

I looked at Eva and Suky who were nodding in agreement with Mum. They had a point, maybe doing magic now wasn't the best idea. But with or without enchantments, the cakes were still delicious. And those CLAWs must be hungry and freezing cold. I chewed my lip thoughtfully, then picked up a tray and made for the door.

Trembling slightly, I pushed the door open with my hip and laid the tray on one of the tables outside.

I cleared my throat.

'Erm,' I began. My voice was weak and shaky and none of the CLAWs even noticed I was there.

'Excuse me,' I tried again.

'SHUT UP!' I bellowed. 'Just for a second. Please!'

There was a shocked silence and twenty heads swivelled round towards me. My bravado deserted me and my legs started to shake.

'I thought you might be hungry.' I took the plates and mugs off the tray and laid them on to the table. Then I scarpered back inside and brought out the other drinks and cakes. The CLAWs were standing still, silently staring at the table.

'Help yourselves,' I said mildly. 'It's on the house.'

Backing away from them I hurried through the door and locked it. Mum, Eva and Suky were sitting on one of the sofas and I collapsed down next to them, giggling with nerves.

'Do you think it'll work?' I asked.

Mum nodded towards the door. The noise level had dropped and I could see one or two of the women had put their placards down and were moving towards the table.

As we watched, more of them took mugs of coffee and soon they were all standing around chatting, munching on the cup cakes and drinking coffee. All thoughts of placards or chanting forgotten – at least for the moment. Though I knew this was only keeping the problem at bay for now – we hadn't made it go away – I couldn't help feeling relieved.

Chapter 33

Mum, Eva and I stood by the window peeking out and smiling to ourselves. The women looked like they were having fun despite the rain, clasping their cold fingers round the warm mugs and laughing over the cakes. Millicent was at the back of the crowd, slightly apart from her groupies. Her face was serious and her eyes dark but from a distance it was impossible to tell what she was thinking. While the ladies gossiped, she turned sharply and strode off back towards town, leaving one latte and one cupcake left untouched on the table.

Mum raised her eyebrows at me and I sniggered. We'd beaten them with a snack.

Once Millicent, who I assumed was their leader, had gone, the other woman started to leave, too. They put their empty mugs back on the table and drifted off along the beach, or back into town, until the only people left were us.

I linked my arm through Mum's.

'No magic needed,' I said gleefully.

Mum squeezed me close.

'For now,' she warned. 'I don't think it'll be that easy next time.'

I waved off her worries. We could fret about that later. Full of beans I turned to see what Suky was doing and gasped in horror. She was slumped on the sofa, eyes closed, her breathing shallow.

As one, Mum, Eva and I raced to her side. Her eyes flickered open for a second, then closed again. Mum cradled her sister like a baby.

'Suky,' she said. 'Suky sweetheart, please talk to me.'

'Get help!' Eva shouted at me, pushing me towards the door. 'Go now. Get Jamie!'

I hesitated for a fraction of a second.

'Go!' Mum and Eva yelled together. So I went.

Chapter 34

Jamie was locking up his surgery when I arrived, panting from running up the hill. I grabbed his arm.

'Come quick,' I gasped. 'It's Suky. She's at the café.'

He didn't stop to ask questions, just bundled me into his car and headed towards the loch. When we arrived outside Suky was sitting up on the sofa and sipping a glass of water. She was horribly pale and wrapped in mum's pashmina. Smiling weakly at us, she coughed a terrible, hacking cough.

Jamie listened to her chest and spoke quietly to her as Mum, Eva and I huddled in the corner and watched. I was shaking with fright and terrified something awful had happened.

'You've got a chest infection,' Jamie said gently, sitting down on the sofa next to Suky. 'I need to give you antibiotics and speak to your oncologist.'

Suky looked relieved.

'I was so scared,' she said in a shaky voice. 'I thought this was it.' She tried to laugh but her voice wobbled.

'It's not completely straightforward,' Jamie said, patting her hand. My heart sang with gratitude to him. 'You'll have to stop your radiotherapy for now.'

'No,' Suky said. 'I can't stop. It's nearly over.'

'They won't do it if they think you're ill,' Jamie said gently.

'Of course I'm ill, I've got cancer,' Suky said. 'Tell them they have to do it.' She looked panicky. 'I don't want to drag it out.'

Jamie looked at Mum for help. She sat down next to her sister and rearranged her pashmina round Suky's shoulders. 'We'll talk about this later,' she said. 'No need to worry now. We should get home.'

We all bundled into Jamie's Land Rover and he drove us up the hill. Harry was there and I briefly wondered where she'd been. She was horrified when she saw how pale Suky was. As we helped Suky up the stairs, she snapped at me.

'I'll take it from here,' she whispered over the top of Suky's head. 'Mum left me a note saying you'd told her to go for a walk. What did you do that for?'

'I thought it might help,' I said. 'Can I give you a hand getting her into bed?'

'I think you've done enough,' Harry snapped. She steered Suky into her bedroom and shut the door.

Hurt, I left her to it. Downstairs, Jamie was hovering in the hall, so I showed him to the door.

'Thanks so much.' I leaned against the doorframe, suddenly feeling exhausted.

Jamie smiled and softly touched my arm, just above my elbow. 'She'll be OK,' he said. 'How are you doing?'

His unexpected kindness made me cry.

'I'm sorry,' I said, sniffing in a most unladylike way and wiping away my tears with the back of my hand. 'It's just been a crazy day.'

Jamie turned on his heel and disappeared back into the kitchen. Confused, I watched him go. When he came back he was holding my coat and my bag.

'Here you are.' He thrust them at me. 'I'm taking you out for dinner.'

That was most definitely not what I had expected. I grinned at him.

'Where are you taking me?' I asked as I shrugged my coat on. Loch Claddach was hardly a hot bed of top restaurants.

'Curry.' Jamie pushed me out of the door and into his car. 'Never let it be said that I don't know how to treat a lady.'

'That is exactly what I need,' I grinned as we headed down the hill. And it really was. Several poppadoms, a chicken tikka masala, one pint of lager and lots of laughter later I felt much better. The horror of Suky's illness and the shock of the locals' campaign against us had receded as Jamie entertained me with tales of his travels and his more eccentric patients.

I leaned back in my chair and rested my hands on my stomach.

'I'm stuffed,' I sighed. 'I need to walk off all this food.'

Jamie signalled the waiter and asked for the bill.

'I'll walk you up the hill,' he said as he waved off my attempts to pay for my share of the curry. 'I can leave my car in town and pick it up tomorrow.'

I didn't protest as I normally would. I was still spooked by today's events and worried some of those frightening women could be lurking about outside our house again. Plus, I couldn't disguise how much I was enjoying Jamie's company.

As we strolled up the hill, I looped my arm through Jamie's. It felt so comfortable to be with him – just like old times really. He was talking about his plans to extend the surgery, but I wasn't really listening. Instead I was admiring his profile. He'd been handsome at school but now he was really gorgeous, I thought to myself. I wondered if tonight had been a date and if he'd try to kiss me when we reached the house. He had lovely lips.

'Don't you agree?' Jamie looked down at me.

'Lips,' I said without thinking. No, that wasn't right. What had he asked me? I had no idea. I smiled at him in what I hoped was a winning way.

'I'm sorry, I didn't catch that,' I said politely.

Jamie laughed.

'I didn't think you were listening,' he chuckled. 'What were you thinking about?'

'Erm, Suky,' I said, hating myself for not thinking about my sick aunt.

Jamie slung his arm around my shoulders and hugged me close.

'The prognosis is good,' he said. 'Putting off the radiotherapy might delay things a bit and she's in for a rough old ride, but I'm really confident she'll get through it. She's very strong.'

I leaned into him as we walked.

'I know,' I said. 'It's just hard to see her like this.'

We'd reached my gate so I paused, turning to face Jamie.

'I had a really nice time,' I said, butterflies flapping madly in my (slightly bloated) stomach. I tilted my head so I'd be ready if he went for the kiss.

'Me too.' He leant down. This was it! A brief worry about chicken tikka breath flashed across my mind but I dismissed it, stepping closer to Jamie.

And then he kissed me on the cheek.

'I'll call you tomorrow,' he said. 'Sleep well.'

And he walked off down the hill.

Chapter 35

I woke up the next morning filled with shame. Suky was fighting for her life, Dom hadn't been gone from my life for five minutes, and all I cared about was locking lips with my ex-boyfriend.

I rolled out of bed and nervously went to find Harry, hoping she wasn't still blaming me for Suky's troubles yesterday.

She came out of her room as I was walking past.

'Sorry about being such a bitch yesterday,' she said immediately. 'I was just so worried.'

'That's OK,' I said. 'I was worried too.'

We walked downstairs and into the kitchen where mum was spreading marmalade on a slice of toast.

I took it from her as I passed, bit into it, then gave it back.

'I rang Brent and told him we didn't need him today,' Mum said, waving off my attempts to get another bite. 'He's got a real bee in his bonnet about the café. He thinks we should close for a while.'

I huffed.

'He's being a bit of a drama queen about it,' I said. 'And he doesn't even know what happened yesterday yet.'

'What happened yesterday?' Harry asked.

'I forgot you missed it all,' I said. 'It was awful.'

I told her about the Housewives' Guild and their placards.

'They've got a name?' she said.

'Oh yes,' I said. 'They're called the CLAWs.'

'That's a rubbish name,' said Harry. She had a point but I couldn't see that it mattered much.

'Brent thinks it's all over for us here,' I said.

Harry snorted.

'What does Nell say about it all?'

Nell! I'd forgotten all about our secret weapon.

'I haven't spoken to her,' I said. I quickly bashed out a text asking her to meet us at the café and she replied immediately.

'She's going there now,' I said. 'Let's go.'

'Where were you yesterday?' I asked Harry as we walked down the hill.

'Just doing some bits,' she said.

'What bits?'

'Why do you care?'

'I just wondered if you were experimenting,' I said.

'With what?' Harry pulled her hat further down on her head. 'God, this wind is terrible.'

'Dark magic,' I said. I'd been doing a lot of research of my own and discovered there was only one branch of magic powerful enough to control life and death. 'Voodoo.'

Harry looked at me sharply.

'Has Mum said anything to you?'

'A bit,' I said. 'Just that you were looking into some things.'

'It's not what you think it is,' she said. 'There are lots of different kinds of voodoo. It's not all chickens' feet and dolls with pins in, you know.'

We were nearing the café and I could see Nell waiting outside, so I dropped it.

'Be careful, H,' I said. But she didn't reply.

162

Chapter 36

'Nothing?' I said, in disbelief. 'Nothing at all?'

Nell shook her head.

'Millicent ran the meeting – she's the chairwoman – and they talked about the Christmas craft fair, who's going to turn on the town lights and whether they'd had any luck in getting a sponsor for the Hogmanay celebrations,' she said.

'But they were all here, yesterday,' I said.

'I know,' Nell said. She looked a bit shamefaced. 'I don't think that's anything to do with Millicent.'

'Hang on,' I said. 'You were adamant. You said she was horrible.'

'I know,' Nell said. 'But I went round for dinner last night and she was really nice to me.'

'You went for dinner?' I said, surprised. 'With Mean Girl Imogen?'

'She's actually quite nice. She was never the cause of all my troubles,' Nell said. 'I think she's been bullied too. She's got bulimia, you know.'

'Really?' I said in surprise. 'Poor girl. I hope she's getting some help.'

I opened a box of teabags and started putting them into a jar to display on the counter.

'But I still think it's Millicent. There's no one else they'd listen to like they listen to her.'

'I think there is someone,' Nell said. 'But I don't know who. After the meeting, some of them – that woman from the chemist and some others – went off together. Millicent didn't go.'

'She's right,' Harry said. 'Groups don't just come together like that. There must be someone behind the scenes, pulling the strings.'

'You can find out who it is,' I said, with a flash of excitement. 'We'll go to the chemist and speak to Stringy Hair, and you can do your Jedi mind trick and get her to tell us who's behind it all.'

'That could work,' Harry said.

'What's a Jedi mind trick?' Nell asked. 'Is it a witchy thing?'

So she did know everything. And she obviously didn't mind.

Harry looked at her.

'It is,' she said gravely. 'But you must never talk about it.'

Nell nodded, her pretty young face serious.

'I'm brilliant at keeping secrets,' she said. The thought of the secrets she'd kept made me sad.

'Right then,' said Harry. 'No point in messing about. I'm off.'

She picked up her handbag and left without even looking back. I envied her confidence.

Nell and I opened the café, but I wasn't sure why we had bothered. We sat for half an hour waiting for Harry to come back, but not one customer came in.

Eventually, the bell above the door tinkled, and Harry came in. She was pale and stony-faced.

'Can you make me a coffee, Ez?' she said. I leapt up, glad of the opportunity to do something.

Harry took off her coat and hung it up on the empty stand. I handed her the coffee and she slumped on to the sofa next to Nell. I sat down opposite.

'What did you find out?' I asked. 'What is it? Why do you look so upset?'

Harry took a breath.

'It's Brent,' she said.

Chapter 37

I stared at Harry, trying to make sense of what she'd said.

'It's Brent,' she repeated.

'No it's not.' I said. 'I know you've got a thing about him because you can't read him, but really he's nice. He's been taking Suky to hospital, for goodness sake.'

'It's him, Ez,' she said.

She sat up.

'It was easy,' she said. 'That woman in the chemist didn't recognise me. So I just got her talking and the rest just happened.'

'So what did she say?'

Harry slurped her coffee.

'I said I'd heard there had been a bit of a kerfuffle at the café yesterday.'

'Kerfuffle at the café,' Nell said with a chuckle. 'I like that.'

Harry silenced her with a look.

'Sorry,' she said.

'Anyway,' Harry went on. 'She sort of laughed and said it was more of a peaceful protest. I bought painkillers, so then I gave her the money and held on to her hand – it makes it simple to read someone if you're touching them. I asked her what she was protesting about and she said – you'll love this – she said they were protesting about witches.'

I gasped. We'd known that, of course, what with their CLAW banners, but it just sounded so brutal when Harry said it.

'So I said who was behind the protests, expecting her to say it was that Millicent,' Harry said. 'And she said, Brent.'

'But she didn't mean our Brent,' I said, still refusing to believe it.

'No she meant the other Brent,' Harry said.

'No need to be sarky,' I said. 'Maybe she meant our Brent, but she didn't mean he was leading it all. Because it's Millicent who's leading it all.'

'Oh give it up, Ez,' Harry said. 'It's not Millicent. It's Brent. And we've let him into our lives – he's got close to you and Suky, he's been going through my accounts for pity's sake, he's got your mum's email passwords. He could be doing anything. Clearing our bloody bank accounts, probably.'

'But why would he do that?' I was still bewildered. How could it be Brent? He was so nice.

Harry looked around the empty café.

'I don't know,' she said. 'But it's working isn't it? I'm going to find him.'

'Oh Harry, no,' I said. 'Wait until we're sure.'

She looked at me with barely controlled anger.

'I'm sure,' she said. 'I know what I heard.'

She pulled her coat off the stand, and marched to the door.

'I'm not going to let him get away with this,' she said.

The door slammed behind her and I looked at Nell.

'What shall we do?' she said.

'I don't know.' I put my head in my hands. 'I am completely out of ideas.'

In the end what we did was shut the café. There was no point in keeping it open if there were no customers, so I locked up and said goodbye to Nell. I didn't want to go home so instead I headed down to the beach. It had started raining, again, so wanting shelter, I headed to the cave.

I sat in the entrance, on the sandy floor, protected from the worst of the wind by the rock and gazed out to sea. I couldn't believe some random man had taken against us so violently that it could cost us our business and our home. What had we ever done to hurt him?

I thought back over all my conversations with Brent and the questions he'd been asking about the café. Hadn't he said his first business was property? Real estate, as he called it? Could this just be about money?

A noise behind the rock made me jump, and I looked up as Jamie appeared. He was wearing a suit and carrying his doctor's bag.

'You're not dressed for the beach,' I said.

'I've just finished my house calls,' he said with a grin. 'I saw Nell and she said you'd come down here and might need some company.'

I smiled and made room for him on the sand.

'Pull up a chair,' I said.

Jamie sat down. I liked the feeling of him so close to me.

'What's up?' he said. 'Why have you closed the café?'

'No customers,' I said. 'They've all turned against us.'

'I'm sure that's not true,' he said.

'Oh it's true all right,' I said. 'Brent's had a hand in it.'

'Brent?' Jamie said. 'No, surely not. He's a nice guy.'

'Been showing him your accounts have you?' I asked.

'I have actually,' Jamie said.

I nodded.

'I think he's been nosing round all the businesses in town, checking out which ones are the most lucrative. We've obviously come out top.'

Jamie looked a bit offended.

'The practice makes money,' he said.

I smiled at his defence of his dad's surgery.

'I think it's our land that makes us the lucky ones,' I said. 'You can't build on the shores of the loch now, can you? We're the only business with that location and that view. And it's never going to change. I expect our building is worth quite a bit.'

Jamie looked bewildered.

'So you think Brent's been snooping around trying to find a money-making scheme?' he said.

'I don't know why he wants it but I think he wants property here,' I said. 'He pinpointed us, but he knew we wouldn't sell so he's had to play dirty.'

Jamie looked stern.

'What's he done?'

'He's got a campaign against us,' I said wearily, leaning back against a rock and hugging my freezing legs. 'He's got the whole village involved and he wants to shut us down.'

'So what are we going to do about it?'

I smiled at the 'we' but I couldn't help shaking my head.

'I'm not sure there's anything we can do,' I said. 'Suky's so ill and Mum and Eva are knackered and Harry's just angry. Maybe it's best just to shut up shop, at least for now.'

'No bloody way!'

I'd never seen laid-back Jamie so riled before. I stared at him in surprise.

'You're not giving up!'

I felt tears come into my eyes – again – and I couldn't speak for a moment.

'Ez, I'm serious.' Jamie took my hand, his blue eyes creased with worry. 'Who's the bravest person you know?'

'Suky I guess,' I said. 'Or my dad.' Thinking about my dad made me want to cry again. 'He's really brave.'

'And what has he done that's so brave?' Jamie said.

'Oh you know, just little things,' I said, with a small smile. 'He fought in a war. He saw his friends killed. And then he was injured so badly that he had to give up the career he loved and build a new life for himself.'

'Did he ever give up?' Jamie asked.

Feeling slightly like a naughty toddler, I shook my head.

'And what about you? It would have been much easier for him to walk away and never get to know you. But did he ever give up on you?'

I shook my head again.

'Exactly!' Jamie was triumphant. 'And that's why you can't give up on this now.'

'But it's so hard,' I whispered.

'But I'm here to help,' Jamie put his arm round me and for a moment I relaxed against him. It felt nice.

'And there's Chloé and Harry. We'll all pitch in.'

'Do you think it'll work?'

'I don't know,' Jamie said. 'But I do know we shouldn't just roll over and let Brent win. We're better than that, Ez. We're braver than that.'

'Come on then, William Wallace.' I heaved myself up and brushed the soggy sand from my bottom. 'Let's go and get a coffee.'

Chapter 38

As we trudged up the street, my phone rang. It was Harry.

'I can't find the bugger,' she said. 'Have you seen him?'

'No,' I said. 'But I haven't been looking.'

Harry sighed impatiently.

'I really want to speak to him, Ez,' she said. 'I need to know what he's playing at.'

'I think it's all to do with money,' I said. I explained my theory again.

'That makes sense,' Harry said. 'So you don't think he's like a modern-day Witchfinder General?'

'I think the witch thing is neither here nor there for him,' I admitted, talking quietly so Jamie wouldn't hear. 'I think he heard some people talking about being a bit dissatisfied with Suky's spells and he just seized the opportunity.'

'What a smoothie he is,' Harry said. She sounded almost impressed. 'He won our trust and used it against us.'

'That's why it makes me feel so sick,' I said.

'I know,' she said sympathetically. 'Me too. Listen, I have some stuff to do for Mum, will you be OK this afternoon?'

'What stuff?' I said.

'Just stuff,' she said, evasively.

170

'Voodoo?'

'Nothing creepy,' she said. 'It's just if we're going to do it, we need to do it on Halloween and that's just a few days away now.'

'Fine,' I said. 'Do your thing.'

I said goodbye and rang off, then I walked across the road to where Jamie had wandered. He was standing staring at a bold poster, slapped, slightly skewwhiff, on to a lamppost.

'Look at this, Esme,' he said.

PROTECT YOUR CHILDREN! the poster read.

'What the bloody hell is this?' I pulled Jamie's arm and looked closer. At the bottom of the poster was a date – Halloween – a time – 7.30pm – a location – St Columba's church hall – and a tiny CLAW logo.

Annoyed and scared I pulled it off the wall and stuffed it into the pocket of my fleece. But as we walked on, I realised we were fighting a losing battle – there were posters everywhere, each with a more sinister slogan than the last.

DO YOU KNOW WHERE YOUR CHILDREN ARE? one read.

WHO'S WATCHING YOU? said another. And each one had the same date on – Brent was definitely planning something.

Jamie was furious and I was confused and upset as we whirled around town pulling down posters as fast as we could. Eventually, clutching a pile of the hateful flyers, we reached the café.

I was relieved to see Mum had opened up again, and even more pleased to see that though there were only a few customers inside, they were Chloë, Rob and the kids.

'What's happened?' she said, as Jamie headed to the counter – and I slumped down next to her, giving Matilda a kiss.

I threw the posters on to the table and spread them out to show them both.

'It's Brent,' I said. 'He's determined to shut us down.'

'Brent?' Chloë said in surprise. 'He's so nice.'

'Long story,' I said.

'So what you gonna do about it,' Rob asked.

I shrugged. All my fight had gone to the counter with Jamie.

'I just don't know.' I looked over at Mum, who was smiling as she made Jamie's coffee. Suddenly I felt close to tears.

'Jamie thinks we can beat him but I don't know,' I said, my voice cracking.

Oliver put his little hand on my cheek.

'Sad?' he said.

I forced myself to smile at him.

'No, darling,' I said. 'Esme is just a silly billy.' I made a face at him and he giggled.

Chloë picked up one of the posters and read it, a look of disdain on her pretty face.

'We're going to take him on,' she said forcefully. 'Rob will help us. We can beat this, Ez.'

I looked at her doubtfully. Brent had been so clever so far, I couldn't see a way out of his tricks.

'Can we?'

'Can we what?'

Jamie squeezed on to the sofa and took Matilda on to his knee. She snuggled into him happily and my heart melted. Honestly, I had to get a grip.

Over her shoulder, he peered at the poster.

'Ah,' he said.

'What does "Ah" mean?' I asked, slightly crossly. I was annoyed with him for being so perfect and making me fancy him.

'It means I think we can take him on,' he said. 'I really think we can do it. We can't just let him get away with it, can we?'

Chloë grinned triumphantly.

'Exactly!'

Seemingly from nowhere she produced a pen and a piece of paper.

'We need a plan,' she declared. 'Let's get on with it.'

Chapter 39

In the end, though, despite the combined efforts of Chloë, Jamie, Rob and me, the plan – or at least the first bit of it – came from an unexpected place – Allan.

He was a quiet, watchful man and, to be brutally honest, apart from when he'd offered Harry and me his studio for my magic lessons, I'd barely ever spoken to him. He and Eva had a happy, calm marriage and as far as I could tell he was very nice. He was as much a part of the scenery of Claddach to me as Mum or Suky.

Anyway, he'd become part of our family and each morning I waved cheerily as he did his Tai Chi on the lawn, and we exchanged pleasantries when our paths crossed, but we'd never shared any jokes or secrets. So it was with a certain amount of surprise that I greeted him when he approached me in the kitchen at home, later that day.

'I thought you might like to have a look at these.' He handed me a bundle of papers.

I had been cooking dinner, so I turned the heat down on the pasta sauce and sat at the table, leafing through the papers. They were more posters – only this time they were adverts for the café.

BAD DAY? they read.

Or BAD BREAK UP?

Or BAD NEWS?

I rifled through them, faster and faster. Below that was a stylised drawing of a cupcake or a cup of coffee, then more writing.

GOOD FOOD, GOOD TIMES, GOOD FRIENDS AT CLADDACH CAFÉ, it read.

I looked at Allan. He grinned sheepishly.

'I overheard you all talking earlier,' he said. 'I thought maybe we could play Brent's game.'

I hadn't even noticed him in the café, let alone clocked that he was listening to us. But I was very grateful he had. The posters were lovely. I leaned over and kissed him on the cheek.

'Thank you, Allan,' I said. 'This means a lot. I know you're busy with your exhibition coming up.'

'Nice to have a break,' he said gruffly, standing up. 'I've got them on my laptop, so just shout if you need any more.'

As he walked out of the kitchen, Harry walked in.

'What's this?' she asked, leafing through the posters.

I turned the pasta back on.

'We're going to put them up over Brent's posters,' I said. 'We're fighting back.'

Harry snorted.

'We're not fighting very hard,' she said. 'He's not going to care about a few flyers.'

I bristled. I was proud of what we'd done so far.

'It's a start,' I said.

'It's going nowhere,' Harry said.

I turned to look at her. She looked back at me, as if daring me to disagree with her and I caved (damn it – she always intimidated me into giving in).

'What do you suggest then?' I said sulkily.

'We need to confront him,' she said again. 'We need to find out exactly what he's up to. And once we know, we can act. He should know we won't just roll over.'

I took the pasta pan over to the sink and drained it.

'He's horrible, though,' I said. 'He's not going to sit down for a chat.'

Harry had taken the Parmesan out of the fridge. She looked round for the grater and shrugged.

'I just think we need to be braver. We've got all sorts of weapons in our armoury.' She started grating the cheese violently.

'No magic,' I said firmly. Harry didn't answer.

'Harry,' I said. 'No magic.'

There was a pause. Harry grated even more vigorously.

I took the cheese from her and she sighed.

'Fine,' she said. 'Do it your way. But if it doesn't work, you have to let me have a go.'

'It's a deal,' I said.

I smiled at her and she smiled back.

'Ooh, I almost forgot,' she said. 'I thought you might be interested in this.' She picked up the copy of *The Scotsman* that was lying on the table and turned to the legal section.

'Look.' She thrust it towards me. 'What do you think? Interested?'

I looked. And I thought. I was most definitely interested. I just had to make a few calls. Harry winked at me.

'I'm not all bad,' she said. I was starting to believe her.

Chapter 40

The next day, Mum and I opened the café though I couldn't really see the point, while Harry stayed at home to look after Suky. She'd finished her antibiotics and was getting stronger, though she was still very frail. She could get out of bed now, and I enjoyed just sitting with her, chatting about life, love and everything. Mentally though, she was struggling. I knew she was finding it hard to cope with her diagnosis and treatment, and this delay, and I was more worried about her state of mind than her physical health. I couldn't help but brood about what Harry was planning for Halloween. Was she messing about with voodoo? It seemed very risky to me. But Harry was a good witch, and I knew she wouldn't harm her mum.

After our first day 'fighting back', Nell came crashing through the back door, just as I was heating up soup for Suky.

'Flipping heck,' I laughed as I poured chicken noodle into a mug. 'How did you get on?'

Nell had somehow managed to befriend Stringy Hair and had tagged along to one of the Housewives' Guild's breakaway meetings with Brent in charge.

'Brilliant,' she said.

'Hold on,' I said. 'I'll just take this up to Suky and I'll be back to hear your news.'

I delivered the soup to Suky, who was dropping with tiredness after being out of bed all day, and when I came back into the kitchen Eva and Mum had arrived. The mood was strangely, given the circumstances, celebrational.

'What's happened?' I asked, suspiciously.

'It's a whispering campaign,' Nell said. 'They're just going to say a few nasty things about us, that's all.'

I slumped on to a kitchen chair, dizzy with relief.

'Are you sure? It seems a bit easy.'

'I'm sure,' Nell said. 'They're just being a bit bitchy, that's all. They're toothless.'

'Toothless CLAWs,' said Eva and she and Mum shrieked with laughter.

I felt uneasy though. Sure we could cope with a few nasty rumours, but Brent seemed more determined than that. And what was this event on Halloween? Were they just going to sit around and say mean things about us?

Sadly, I was right. As the next day passed, the whispers got louder. The café didn't get any busier. It wasn't worth opening really but Mum stubbornly refused to give in. Two days before Halloween, Harry went back to Edinburgh, to sort out some work bits she couldn't do over the internet. As she left she gave me a meaningful glance.

'When I get back, we'll do it my way,' she said. She meant to be reassuring, I think, but it just made me feel even more uneasy.

Worse than the lack of customers at the café, was the bad feeling in town. In a few short days people who had been our friends had turned on us. Some of them whispered on corners and stopped talking when we got near. Most of them just hurried by with an embarrassed half-smile, as if to say they were sorry about what was happening, but didn't want to get involved. And *oh is that the time, I must go and collect the kids* . . . But a small group of women – led by vicious Stringy Hair from the chemist – were becoming openly hostile.

The day Harry went, we ran out of milk at home and I wandered down to the corner shop to buy some more. Stringy Hair was in there, chatting with the shop assistant and a couple of other women. Hating myself for feeling intimidated, I took a pint of milk out of the fridge and put it on the counter. The women stopped talking and stared at me.

'Just this please,' I said in a cheerful, if slightly shaky, voice.

There was a pause, then slowly and deliberately, all three women turned their backs on me. I stood and looked at them for a moment, not sure what to do. They didn't move. So I left the milk on the counter and rushed out of the shop.

The one bright spot in all this was Jamie. He popped by every day to see how Suky was feeling. Then he'd sit with me for a while and chat about his day and listen to my worries about Brent. I found myself looking forward to his visits and even –in my unguarded moments – daydreaming about what would happen if my enchantment had actually worked. Against my better judgement I couldn't help wishing it had. Or if not, that I could enchant him myself with just the force of my dazzling good looks and sparkling personality. I wasn't hopeful.

After the milk incident I let myself into the house and leant wearily against the front door, gathering my thoughts before I faced Mum. Jamie came down the stairs and stopped when he saw my white face.

'You look like you need a cup of tea,' he said.

I managed a weak smile.

'There's no milk.'

'Wine, then,' Jamie said. 'There's always wine in this house.'

I giggled, despite the horrible day I'd had.

'It's not even lunchtime,' I said.

Jamie screwed up his face.

'Ah, you're right,' he said. 'In that case, lovely lady, I will return later.'

And true to his word, he did. He came back that evening with a pint of milk and a bottle of Pinot Grigio.

We sat in the living room, side by side on the sofa, and wrote a list of ideas to get rid of Brent. They ranged from telling immigration he was here illegally, to persuading him there was a monster in Loch Claddach like the one in Loch Ness, and getting him to go and look for it.

'Honestly,' Jamie said, earnestly. 'Americans love Nessie. He'll be wading in before you know it.'

I giggled, heady with wine and the fact that I was sitting with Jamie and we weren't hating each other.

Jamie was watching me, a small smile on his lips.

'What?' I said.

'You're so sweet,' he said. Was it my imagination or was his leg pressing against mine? I made a face at him. Sweet was not a description I liked.

'Don't be patronising,' I said, slightly sniffily. The pressure on my thigh eased a bit. I shifted so I was closer to him again.

'I just mean that you really care about your family,' Jamie said. He leaned his head back on the sofa cushions and looked at me sideways. 'It's nice, that's all.'

I threw my head back, too.

'Well, they're nice,' I said. 'I just want things to be OK.' I lolled my head sideways so I was facing him.

'I haven't always been very supportive. I'm kind of making up for stuff I did a long time ago.'

Jamie tilted his head towards mine.

'Is that why you're being so nice to me?' he asked. His face was close to mine.

'Nope,' I said with a smile. 'That's because you're being so nice to me.'

His kiss, when it came, was just as I remembered, only without the timidity of teenage snogs. It felt exactly right and I wondered why I'd ever wasted more than a decade not kissing him. But as I relaxed into the kiss, doubts crowded into my mind. Even though this time I knew there had been no love spells involved, the fact was, if I got too close to Jamie I'd have to tell him the truth about us. He was a doctor, for heaven's sake, a scientist; I just couldn't see how we could ever have a future.

Pushing him away, I stood up.

'I can't, Jamie.'

He stood up too and took my hands.

'What's the matter?'

I wondered what he would do if I told him the truth. For a moment I thought it might work, that me being a witch wouldn't matter. Then I came to my senses.

'I'm so sorry,' I said. Then I turned and walked away.

Chapter 41

The next day was horrible. I couldn't stop thinking about the look on Jamie's face when I left him. My mind was racing and I couldn't make sense of my feelings.

Thankfully, Harry arrived back, all guns blazing and determined to take Brent on. Suddenly I had something else to worry about, and my concerns about Jamie had to be put to one side.

'It's Sunday,' I said as Harry plotted her approach. 'So he's bound to be at home – there's not much to do in Claddach on a Sunday.'

I hadn't seen anything of Brent since we found out he was behind the campaign and we hadn't heard from him either. Now I wondered if he knew we knew.

'I'll text him,' Harry said. 'I'll pretend I want some advice about the spa. I've got some new bits I can show him actually.'

I eyed her suspiciously.

'You know you're not actually getting business advice from him?'

'Well, yes,' she said. 'But if it's a way into the conversation then I'm not too proud to ask. And if it's useful advice then so much the better.'

I gave up. I didn't even bother trying to talk Harry round. I knew better than to take her on when she was in this sort of mood. Instead I just shrugged. I was so heartbroken over Jamie that I was past caring.

Harry marched off down the hill towards the flat that Brent was renting and I dragged myself into the living room, where I lay on the couch and watched *Come Dine with Me* repeats. Eventually, what felt like hours later, the door slammed and Harry came in.

She shoved my legs out of the way and sat down on the couch, her face like thunder.

'What happened?' I asked, turning off the TV.

'That man is an arse.' Harry said.

'Well, obviously,' I said, but slightly upset that he'd taken me in so thoroughly. 'What did he do?'

Harry harrumphed.

'He made a pass at me,' she said.

I stared at her, open-mouthed.

'No. Way.'

'Way.' Harry shook her head. 'Why do men always try it on with me?'

I had an idea it was to do with her shiny hair, long legs, curvy figure and perfect skin, but I kept quiet. Instead I patted her hand reassuringly.

'He was quite frosty at first,' she continued. 'I wondered if he'd heard that we knew.'

'Do you think he does?' I asked. 'If he knows, we've lost the element of surprise.'

'I'm not sure even that can help us now,' Harry pointed out. 'Anyway, I piled on the charm and did my thing, you know.'

'Did it work?' I asked, remembering how tricky she'd found it to read his aura.

Harry made a so-so gesture with her hand.

'A bit,' she said. 'He started to open up and tell me about how he'd been putting feelers out for businesses here, but I couldn't keep it up. So in the end I gave up. I swear he sensed weakness and thought he may as well have a go.'

I made a face.

'So anyway, I told him I was gay . . .'

'Woah,' I interrupted. 'How did he take that?'

Harry grimaced.

'Not great,' she said. 'He asked me if I was sure. Then he told me I was too pretty to be a lesbian. Then he tried to kiss me again.'

'God loves a trier,' I said. 'Why didn't you do some magic?'

Harry wasn't having that.

'Because you told me not to,' she said.

I shrugged. She had a point.

'So how did you leave it with him?'

'Not good. He was really put out. I can't imagine anyone says no to him very often – women or men,' Harry sighed. 'Oh Ez, I think confronting him might have made things worse. He's bound to realise we're on to him now and step up his game.'

I felt like I had nothing left to lose. Our home and our business were under threat, Dom was back with Rebecca, I'd pushed Jamie away . . . It was my turn to try.

'Is he still there?' I asked. 'Still at his place?'

Harry nodded.

'I guess so,' she said.

'I'm going.'

'Really?' Harry said, doubt etched on her face. 'Is that a good idea?

'I don't care,' I said. I picked up my coat. 'I'll be back in a bit.'

Chapter 42

Brent's flat was right on the town square, above one of the tourist tat shops. I averted my eyes from the Nessie hats – they only made me think of Jamie. I rang the old-fashioned pull bell then realised there was a new buzzer, so I rang that as well and waited for him to answer. He didn't speak, just buzzed me in. I climbed the stone stairs nervously – he'd opened the front door so I went right in.

Brent was sitting in an armchair, drinking a glass of whisky.

'I thought you'd come,' he said. 'Have a seat.'

'No thanks,' I said, then regretted it and sat down anyway.

'So, Esme McLeod,' he said. 'What can I do for you?'

'You can start by telling me what you're up to,' I said. 'Why are you doing this to us?'

'Oh Esme, it's nothing personal,' he said. He smiled his perfect smile. 'It's just business.'

'It is not just business,' I said. 'It's our lives.'

He shrugged.

'Time to toughen up, sweetheart.'

'How dare you,' I said, angry now. 'How dare you swan in here and ruin my family?'

'I'm not ruining you,' he said. He looked hurt at the suggestion.

'I've just been emailing my lawyer, actually. Tomorrow she'll be in touch to offer your mom and your aunt a not inconsiderable sum to take the café off their hands.'

'But less than you'd have to offer if business was booming,' I said.

'Oh you are clever, Esme McLeod,' he said. 'Maybe I'll find a position for you in Portland Property.'

'I wouldn't work for you if my life depended on it,' I said, disgusted.

Brent looked delighted.

'It's going to be a retreat,' he said. 'Hunting, fishing, ceilidhs, you know the sort of thing. The real Scotland. Those guys back home are going to love it.'

He picked up a sheaf of papers.

'I've got the plans here,' he said. 'Do you want to see? There will be five luxury bedrooms, a bar and a restaurant.'

'You'll never get planning permission,' I said.

'Oh but I will,' he said. 'Because I've also looked at the accounts for the garage, and the CCTV at the pub, and I know things about some of your local councillors.' He over-enunciated the unfamiliar word. 'And I've helped the editor of the *Inverness Gazette* with his internet connection and – phew – do I know some things about him that he is not going to want his wife to find out about. So I can rely on his support. It's going to be a real money-spinner. I even asked Millicent Fry if she'd manage it for me, but she turned me down.'

I was impressed.

'She did?'

'I'm still working on her,' Brent confessed. 'She'll come round.'

'You don't have anything to persuade her with?'

Brent looked disappointed.

'Nothing,' he said. 'She's clean as a whistle. That's unusual you know.'

'So what's this big meeting tomorrow night?' I asked.

'Ooh that's the big reveal,' he said. 'I'm going to show all my friends here the plans, and ask if I can count on their support.'

'What's with the posters then?' I said, puzzled.

'And I'm also going to get them to force you out of town,' he said conversationally. 'They're all so scared since I suggested you might be witches, that they won't take much persuasion. And then on Tuesday, you'll receive a much lower offer for the café.'

I had heard enough.

'You have chosen the wrong family to mess with,' I told him, standing up to leave.

'Yeah, yeah,' he said as I opened the front door. 'Try harder, baby, I'm not scared of you.'

I was furious, and spoke without thinking.

'Yeah well you should be,' I spat. 'You know those stories about witches? They're all true.'

His laughter followed me down the street.

Harry was right when she said she'd thought her altercation with Brent would make things worse. Or maybe it was mine. Or both. Who knows?

Chapter 43

Monday morning started out badly when the letterbox rattled first thing. Harry went to the door, thinking – of course – it would be the postman. But it was a hand-delivered, tatty-looking, padded envelope with nothing written on it. She tore it open and recoiled in disgust.

Holding it at arm's length, she opened the front door and threw it out. Mum and I watched her in surprise.

'What on earth . . .' Mum started.

Harry gagged.

'Dog shit,' she said. 'God, that's disgusting.'

Mum put her hand to her mouth.

'Why would anyone . . .' She trailed off, obviously unable to take it in.

I was furious.

'This has gone too far,' I hissed, putting my arm around Mum. 'We need to stop it.'

I guided Mum back into the kitchen and put the kettle on. Harry sat on the work surface, her dark eyes clouded with anger.

'We need to find out what's going on,' she said. 'Something's changed.'

What had changed, we found out later, was that Brent, who was obviously still stewing about Harry's knock-back, had whipped his CLAWs up into such a frenzy that – to please him, I guess – they'd decided to up their game.

Mum and I sat at the kitchen table, huddled over our cups of tea.

'Don't tell Suky.' Mum stared into her mug as though she was telling her own fortune.

'Of course not.' I was slightly cross she even thought we would consider it. 'What about Eva?'

'I'll tell her now.' Mum drained her tea. 'Can you open the café?'

I gawped at her.

'Seriously?'

She shrugged.

'I'm not really sure what else to do.' Her voice cracked on the last word and she swallowed, then pulled herself together and spoke brightly.

'Right then, let's get on.' She kissed the top of my head, pulled her jacket from the hook and disappeared out of the back door to find Eva. Harry went upstairs to see her mum and I was alone.

Slowly, I got up, put on my boots and my coat and, winding my scarf round my neck, I left the house. I averted my eyes as I walked past the soiled envelope; even thinking about it made me feel sick.

As I walked, I thought about ringing Jamie. I wasn't sure what to say but I dialled his number anyway. I was relieved though to find his mobile was switched off and I couldn't think what to say on a message.

'Hi, it's me. Just wanted to let you know someone sent us dog poo in the post. Call me back!'

Perhaps not.

I wasn't really paying attention to my surroundings, so it was a surprise when a stone scuttled across the pavement in front of me as I walked, narrowly missing my leg. I glanced round, instinctively, and caught sight of some young teenage boys skulking in front of the chemist. Had they thrown it? Surely not. But they were all staring at me in a defiant way and I had to walk right by them.

Fishing in my bag, I pulled my phone out again and pretended to answer a call, just so I would look busy. But they weren't fooled. As I walked by one of them, an unpleasant looking lad, wearing a too-small Hollister hoodie, made a noise deep in his throat. Knowing he was going to spit at me, I checked for a gap in the (non-existent) traffic and sprinted across the road, still pretending to chat on my phone.

'I know!' I said, gaily, desperately making out I hadn't seen them. 'It was sooooo funny!'

And then my phone rang.

The boys' laughter echoed round the town, as I took to my heels and ran away.

Chapter 44

All morning I sat in the deserted café, hoping for a customer but jumping every time I heard a noise. There was no sign of the CLAWs – they were probably all preparing for tonight's meeting – and though I thought I saw Brent running down by the loch, I wasn't absolutely sure it was him.

I cleaned the café from top to bottom. With my actual hands, not magic. Then I sat on the counter, swinging my legs like I used to do when I was younger. Looking round at the business my mum had built up, I remembered how it must have looked just a few weeks earlier. Warm and cosy, the windows steamed up, noisy with chatter and the froth of the coffee machine. A safe haven.

Jumping down from my perch, I walked listlessly to the window and wiped off the condensation to peer out. It was raining and there was no one about.

Chewing my lip, I stood up and gazed out over the loch. The café was a solid, stone building, decades older than the local laws that forbade building on the shores of the loch. The views from the large windows were breathtaking. And though we only used the top floor for storage, it was ripe for conversion. It would make a perfect, quaint hotel. There was hiking, shooting and fishing on the doorstep – all things guaranteed to appeal to his target audience. Suddenly everything seemed clear. And completely hopeless.

Then I tried to ring Jamie – again. And got his voicemail – again.

Nell appeared at my side – I hadn't even noticed her coming in.

'Hi,' I said.

She squeezed my arm sympathetically.

'What are you going to do?' She stared at me, a worried look on her face.

I shrugged.

'Go home, I suppose,' I said. 'Back to London.'

'What about your mum? And Eva? And what will Suky do?'

'I don't know,' I snapped. 'I don't know anything.'

I put my head in my hands feeling useless. I couldn't understand how everything had gone so wrong. Just a month ago I'd had a fabulous job, a handsome boyfriend (sort of) and a loving family with a thriving business. Now I'd lost my boyfriend, pissed off the only man to treat me nicely for about a decade and ruined my family's business. Well done, Esme. Nice one.

The door opened and I looked up. Mum, Eva and Allan stood there.

'We felt we should all be together,' Mum said.

I snorted.

'Eat cake while we're hounded out of town?'

Mum put her arm round me.

'Pretty much,' she said.

But I wanted no part of it.

While Mum and Eva enchanted some cupcakes to give us courage in the face of adversity (I snorted again at that one), I stared out of the window and watched groups of women hurrying towards the church hall, where Brent's meeting was being held.

I wasn't sure what was going to happen after the meeting. Would Brent just arrive and announce they'd decided we should leave? Or would they discuss tactics and plan ways to make our lives a misery until we left of our own accord?

'Is Suky all right?' I asked, shaking my head as Mum offered me a cupcake, then changing my mind and taking one anyway.

'She was sleeping when we left,' Mum said. 'Harry knows where we are. She was in a right old mood. She was making lots of notes in her spell book. Lord only knows what she's up to.'

I groaned. I had a good idea. In fact I wasn't sure whether to be worried that Harry would experiment with the voodoo she claimed was good to help her mum, or dabble with more sinister black magic and try it out on Brent.

We were all quiet. Digging my own spell book out of my bag, I began leafing through it, looking for anything that might help our situation. Mum wiped down the counter. Eva and Allan sat on the sofa chatting quietly and Nell drummed out an unheard rhythm on a cushion. Outside it had started raining.

'I got the email with the offer,' Mum said suddenly.

'How much is it?'

Mum shrugged.

'A lot,' she admitted. 'But not nearly enough when you think about what it's worth.'

There was silence as we all looked at each other.

'You're not really going to leave are you?' I said.

Mum and Eva glanced at each other.

'No, we're not.' Allan's voice was firm and probably a bit louder than it needed to be. It was so rare for him to speak at all, that I was taken by surprise.

'I refuse to be bullied by some irritating squirt,' he said.

'Squirt?' Nell giggled. Then I giggled. And so did Mum and Eva. Allan looked hurt for a minute, then he laughed too.

Chapter 45

As we all roared with laughter, my phone rang. It was Chloë. Not wanting to break the moment, I cancelled the call. It rang again straight away. I cancelled it again. When it rang a third time, I gave up and answered.

'What's up, Chlo?' I was still chuckling to myself.

'Oh Esme, thank god,' Chloë was breathy.

'What?' My heart started to thump. 'What's happened?'

'I'm at your house.' Chloë sounded like she was going to cry. 'I can't get in, but I can see through the window and Suky's lying on the floor. I've been banging on the front door and the window, but she's not moving. I don't know what to do!'

I was strangely calm.

'Can you see Harry?' I said. 'Harry should be there.'

'I can't see her,' Chloë said. 'Where is she?'

'I don't know,' I wailed. Chloë gasped and I took a breath. 'Right, phone Jamie,' I said firmly. 'We're on our way. Keep knocking on the window, she might wake up.'

Grabbing my bag, I looked at the white faces of the others.

'Suky's in trouble,' I said. 'We need to go.'

Mum had her car at the café, so we all piled in and luckily it started first time. When we arrived, Chloë was pacing the front garden and as we ran up the path, she flew at us, gabbling about what had happened but making no sense.

Mum tried to unlock the door but her hands were shaking too much to get the key in the hole. Instead, Eva reached over her shoulder, waved her hand and we all watched in relief as the door swung open. Then we pushed in to the lounge, where Suky lay curled up on the carpet.

Mum cradled her sister, stroking her hair and talking quietly to her. Suky stirred but she didn't open her eyes. Her breathing was shallow and her skin was grey.

Feeling helpless, I looked around, suddenly realising what had been going on.

The air was heavy with magic. It hung in the room like a cloud of gas, shimmering slightly as though a heat haze had leaked in from outside. On the coffee table was Suky's spell book and several candles. One had been melted and moulded into a figure. I picked it up. There were some hairs pushed into the head that I recognised as Suky's.

'What's this?' I said, showing Eva.

She went pale and crouched by Suky and Mum.

'What have you done, Su?' she whispered.

What Suky had done was a super-powerful spell. She'd tried banishing her cancer, by cursing it out of her. But it was too much magic for one woman, especially one weakened by weeks of radiotherapy. The enchantment was hanging around in the air like a nasty carbon monoxide leak and we had to get rid of it.

I turned to Nell, who was looking pale, scared and very, very young.

'Nell,' I said urgently. 'Can you find Jamie? Tell him we do need him, but try to keep him out of the way for about ten minutes. And see if you can track Harry down.'

We had to try to reverse the spell and I didn't think a bemused onlooker would help.

Nell looked like she was going to ask me a question, then she thought twice.

'Right,' she said and headed out back down the hill.

'What are *we* going to do?' Chloë said. Her freckles stood out on her white face.

'I have absolutely no idea,' I admitted. 'Where's bloody Harry? She'd know what to do.'

'Can't you find her?' Chloë said. 'Tune into her or something?'

I was doubtful, though I knew Harry could always find me when she wanted to.

'I can try,' I said. I closed my eyes and reached out with my mind, just as we'd practised in my magic lessons – and Harry was right there, reaching to me.

'About bloody time,' she said in my head. 'I'm in my room. Hurry.'

I leapt upstairs, two or even three at a time. Harry's bedroom door was closed.

'Esme,' she said from behind the door. 'Mum's up to something. Something bad. She's taken all my voodoo stuff and she did some sort of binding spell to stop me going after her. You have to get me out of here.'

'OK,' I said. 'Stand back.'

I had no idea what to do but somehow my magic just took over. Pink sparks flew from my fingers and the air around Harry's room shimmered and crackled. The door splintered, then opened, and Harry emerged. Her hair was slightly messy but apart from that, she was fine.

'Is your magic back?' I asked. Binding spells could stop witches for weeks, months even.

Harry waved her hand experimentally and we both ducked as sparks flew across the hallway.

'Yes,' she said in relief. 'Mum's so weak, she can't have bound me too tightly.'

She looked at me.

'Where is Mum?' she said, panic in her eyes. 'Is she OK?'

'Harry,' I began, but she was already shoving me out of the way and running downstairs and into the living room.

195

'Mum!' she gasped and went to Suky's side. Cradling her tiny frame, she looked like the mother and I felt so sorry for her. Eyes wide, Harry looked round the room, taking in the magic hanging over our heads.

'Oh shit,' she whispered. 'This is all my fault.'

Mum shushed her briskly, as they lifted Suky's frail body on to the couch.

'Let's not worry about that now,' she said, like an old-fashioned matron. 'Here.'

She passed Harry the blanket that always hung over the back of the sofa and tenderly, Harry tucked it round her mum. She was so pale she looked almost translucent and her breathing was shallow. But she was breathing, that was something. Mum and Eva bustled around, collecting things and talking to each other in low voices.

I was no wiser about what was going on. I cleared my throat.

'What's happening?' I said in a small voice.

Mum looked at me over her shoulder as she arranged candles. 'It's voodoo,' she said. 'Black magic.'

I shivered.

'Is it bad voodoo?' I asked.

Harry looked grim as she hugged her mum.

'It's really bad, Esme. Can't you feel it?'

'Suky has invited spirits into the house,' Mum explained. 'You can do deals with the dead, if you know what you're doing.'

I shivered again, more violently this time. Eva picked up a cardigan that was lying on a chair and wrapped it gently round my shoulders.

'Does Suky . . .' I was scared to even ask the question. 'Does she know what she's doing?'

Eva was tight-lipped as she deftly avoided answering. 'It's dangerous and it's not our kind of magic. I don't know why she thought it could work.'

'It doesn't matter why she did it,' Mum was abrupt. 'She did it.'

I shot a look at Harry. She stroked Suky's hair and didn't meet my eyes.

'We've been researching it for weeks,' she said, her voice quiet. 'We've been reading the Book of Shadows.'

Mum looked shocked.

'Where did you get one of those?'

'You can get anything you want these days,' she said. 'I've got a contact in Haiti.'

'What were you thinking, Harry,' Eva asked. She was looking at Harry as though she'd never seen her before.

'I knew we were playing with fire, but I thought it was worth the risk. Mum wanted to try and I wanted to feel useful.' She let out a long, shuddering breath. 'But all the time I was trying to find a good way of using the magic, Mum was plotting to use a much more powerful – and dangerous – spell. We were about to start the casting when she said she wanted to check something in my room. What a lame excuse – I can't believe I fell for it. As soon as I walked in, she cast the binding spell, grabbed my bag and locked me in.'

She looked down at Suky.

'And now look at her.'

A single tear rolled down her cheek. She didn't wipe it away.

'It's not your fault, H,' I said. 'This wasn't what you meant to happen.'

Chloë was backing towards the door, clearly spooked by the talk of spirits, but Mum held her hand out.

'We need you, my love,' she said. 'This is powerful stuff. We can't do it alone.'

I took Chloë's hand.

'Sorry,' I whispered. She squeezed my fingers.

'Erm,' she sounded very young. 'Can I just . . . It's just . . . Is it dangerous? The kids . . .'

Mum put her arm round her.

'I won't let anything happen to you, Chloë,' I watched her

carefully to check she wasn't lying. Her eyes were clear, though her voice shook. 'We just need more of us working, that's all.'

Together we knelt on the floor by the coffee table. Mum had found a tiny spell book underneath Suky's well-thumbed tome. She put it on the table. It was bound in something that looked like . . .

'Is that skin?' I almost gagged.

Mum nodded grimly and even Harry looked shocked.

'Where did she . .? I didn't get this . . .' she began.

Eva put her hand on Harry's shoulder and she stopped talking.

Mum opened the tiny book. It was crammed full of small writing. She and Eva held hands and exchanged a glance that I couldn't read. Then Mum took my hand and Eva took Harry's and Chloë's. Together Mum and Eva breathed the words written in the book. It was like a cloud had passed over the sun. The room darkened and straight away I felt heavy and hopeless. Chloë was crying, silent tears running down her freckled cheeks. The air in the room was so thick I struggled to breathe, like I'd been on a ten-mile run. Suky moaned and I instinctively went to reach out to her, but Mum held my hand tightly and stopped me with a look.

When they reached the end of the page, the room lightened slightly, but the oppressive feeling stayed. I looked at Suky. She stirred but didn't open her eyes.

Chapter 46

'Did it work?'

Mum shook her head, I could tell she was close to tears. Harry let out a sob. I put my arm round her.

Eva rubbed her forehead, then gently stroked Suky's hair.

'We're not strong enough,' she said.

'Why not?' I said, my voice shrill. 'There are four of us witches here. Why aren't we strong enough?'

Harry's eyes flashed with anger.

'It's Brent, isn't it?' she said. 'Brent's hatred – and the bad feeling of the town – has weakened us.'

Mum nodded.

'I think so,' she said. 'We can't work while there's all this negative energy around. It's just making things worse.'

I thought of the women I'd watched walking into Brent's meeting. The one where, even now, he was probably telling them how we deserved to be driven from our homes and business.

'How much time do we have?' I asked Mum.

She shrugged. 'A while, I guess,' she said, watching Suky. 'She's not getting any worse, for now.'

I tugged at Harry's sleeve.

'Let's go,' I said softly. She knew exactly what I meant. She kissed Suky's forehead and got up. Chloë got up, too.

'I'm coming,' she said.

As we walked down the hill, Jamie and Nell drove past in Jamie's Land Rover. Jamie pulled over when he saw us.

'What's happening?' he said. 'How's Suky?'

'She's not good,' I said, avoiding his eyes. 'Go on up, we've just got to see someone.'

'Who are you going to see? What's going on?'

I looked at my feet.

'I'll explain it all later,' I said. 'Please, just go.'

His face stony, Jamie turned the key and started the car again. Then he drove off without a word. I wondered if that was it between us. I suspected I'd pushed him too far this time.

I stewed over Jamie's grim face as we walked down the hill and by the time we reached the church hall, I was ready for a fight.

We paused outside the hall. My bravado deserted me and I almost turned round, but Harry and Chloë were next to me and I knew they wouldn't let me down.

'I can't do it,' Harry said. I stared at her in surprise. She was never scared. 'It's too important,' she said, starting to cry. I hadn't seen her cry since we were children. 'What if it goes wrong – I can't lose my mum, Ez.'

Chloë looked at me.

'I'll stay with her at the back,' she said. 'You go.' She shoved me towards the door. Gently, but it was definitely a shove.

With my heart pounding, I pushed open the double doors to the church hall and slunk inside. The hall was packed; jammed with just about everyone who lived in Claddach – all the women at least. Every seat was taken and there were women standing at the sides, leaning against the walls, watching Brent. He was on stage, lit by a spotlight in front of a microphone. He looked like he should be singing 'My Way', but instead he was speaking.

'Ladies,' he said. His voice was soft, but I could hear every word.

'This is not the world your children should be growing up in. We need to cut out this cancer and we need to cut it out, now.'

There was a murmur of agreement across the audience.

Brent stood very still until the crowd fell silent once more. Then he straightened up and seemed to loom over the mic. 'Until this family leaves Claddach . . .' He paused. 'Until this whole family goes, we are not safe in our beds.'

Behind him was a white board with the plans for his hotel on it. He was so clever – stirring up bad feeling against us to build his own business. Clever, but evil. The women, though, were lapping it up. They cheered as he spoke.

I gasped. I knew things were bad, but I hadn't realised the strength of feeling against us. Was I stupid to even consider this? Tears filled my eyes and for a second all I could think about was leaving that horrible, claustrophobic hall. I turned back towards the door, then a picture of Suky's pale, thin face filled my mind and I knew I couldn't back out now. I took a step down the aisle, feeling like Johnny coming into Kellerman's at the end of *Dirty Dancing*.

'No one puts Esme in a corner,' I whispered.

I took another step, then another. As I walked between the rows of chairs, heads swivelled towards me. I didn't think I'd ever been so scared but knowing Harry and Chloë were behind me made me feel better.

I walked faster, ignoring the shouts and taunts as I passed. Brent stood still in the centre of the stage and I paused at the small steps leading up, wondering how to get past him.

Harry realised what I was thinking.

'Ez,' she hissed from the back of the hall. I looked at her, and she waggled her fingers gently. Of course.

'How nice of you to join us,' Brent said, looking down at me from the stage. 'Have you come to accept my offer?'

I walked up the three stairs on to the stage. My legs were shaking so violently I wasn't sure I could stand up.

'We won't be accepting your offer,' I said. 'Not today, not tomorrow, not ever. We belong in Claddach and this is where we're staying.'

Someone in the crowd booed. I ignored them.

'So you think we're witches, do you?' I asked Brent. His handsome face was twisted with hatred.

'No,' he said in disdain. 'Of course not. But these women are so gullible they believed the first rumour they heard. They've got no minds of their own. A few whispers and suddenly they're all believing it. After that it was easy.'

Someone else booed. I wondered if this time the abuse was meant for Brent. Claddach women wouldn't like being told they were gullible. The thought made me braver.

'The thing is, Brent,' I said, beginning to waggle my fingers and watching as pink sparks surrounded him. 'The thing is, you were right. We are witches.'

The sparks turned into glittering pink chains and wrapped themselves round Brent. There was a gasp from the crowd, but I couldn't tell if it was approving or disapproving.

'We are witches, and we're very angry with you.'

Brent couldn't move. He was completely wrapped up in enchanted pink chains.

'Get me out of here.' Brent was furious. 'I will have you charged with assault!'

At the front of the crowd, someone stood up. It was Millicent Fry.

'But there are no witnesses,' she said. 'So it would just be your word against Esme's.'

I stared at her, wondering how I could have misjudged her so badly and she winked at me.

'Go on, love,' she said.

My confidence boosted, I stood behind the microphone. The noise from the audience grew as some of the women began pushing their chairs back and standing up, ready to walk out – even though Brent had annoyed them, it didn't mean I was in the clear.

I coughed.

'Erm,' I said, in a tiny voice. 'Excuse me.'

The noise grew and suddenly I was furious. My beloved aunt was lying close to death and barely breathing and these women – who I'd always thought of as our friends – couldn't even stay to hear what I had to say.

'SHUT UP!' I bellowed. The chattering stopped and everyone stood still and gawped at me.

'NOW SIT DOWN!' As one, the women all filed back to their chairs and sat down meekly.

'Thank you,' I said, sounding like a primary school teacher. I felt exposed standing in the spotlight, so slightly awkwardly I took the microphone out of the stand and sat down on the edge of the stage.

'You all know Suky?' I started. 'I know you know her. She's funny and clever and kind and she's helped all of you. And now she needs you to help her.' My voice caught in my throat.

'She's done something really stupid and she's really, really ill. But we can help her. I just need you all. I need you to stop hating us and to just wish us well . . .' I put the microphone down next to me and buried my face in my hands. Was I wasting my time? What could I possibly say to these women that could persuade them to come?

Gathering myself, I saw Mary Barnes in the front row, next to where Millicent was sitting. I picked the mic up again.

'Mary,' I said, ignoring the other women in the room. 'Suky helped you find a new job, didn't she?'

Mary stared at me coldly. I carried on.

'She did.' I knew I had it right. 'You asked her advice and lo and behold your job at the new tourist information centre just fell into your lap, didn't it? I remember.' I met her glance and eventually, reluctantly, she nodded.

Warming up now I scrambled to my feet and pointed at Liz McAdams.

'She cured your morning sickness!' I declared. 'And you, Millie.' I narrowed my eyes at a small tight-lipped woman further back. 'You weren't having much luck with your IVF were you? Until Suky stepped in.' I ignored any guilt I felt at shouting about people's personal problems and carried on, picking audience members at random, and pointing at them wildly, like a TV psychic.

'Your husband doesn't snore anymore! Yours doesn't chase after other women! You have a whole new career! Your brother didn't go to prison for that tiny little embezzlement misunderstanding!'

All around the room, the women were staring at me in horror, and seeing their open-mouthed, desperate looks, I came to my senses.

'Sorry,' I whispered. 'I'm sorry.'

There was a moment, while I stared out at the crowd and they stared back at me. Even Harry and Chloë were watching me. I froze.

Then, at the back of the hall, a chair scraped the floor and someone stood up.

'Suky stopped my daughter being bullied,' said a small voice. I couldn't see who was speaking because the spotlight was too bright. 'She's beautiful and funny but she just couldn't see it. Suky helped her. And I don't think it was magic, or spirits or whatever. It was just friendship.'

'Yay Mum!' Nell shouted – she'd crept into the hall and was standing next to Harry at the back. I blinked in surprise.

And then another chair scraped. Closer to the front this time.

'Suky found my dog,' said Mrs Wilkins, who'd been an old lady when I was a child and didn't seem to have changed in twenty years. 'She walked up and down the beach until she found him.'

Millicent stood up.

'Suky gave me a little tonic to help put the spark back into

204

my marriage,' she said with a cheeky grin. 'I haven't had so much fun in years.'

And then suddenly, there was a cacophony of voices, each telling me of something that Suky had done – just because – that had helped someone. I was overwhelmed by how much love everyone had for my aunt. And for Eva and Mum – there were stories about them, too.

When the noise had died down, I picked up the microphone again. 'Thank you,' I said. 'Thank you for loving us.'

There was a general noise that I took to mean 'you're welcome'.

I walked down the steps and along the aisle and, chattering loudly, the women shuffled along the rows of chairs and followed me out. The meeting was over.

As I reached the door, Millicent called out to me.

'Esme? What shall we do with Brent?'

I looked over to where Brent stood, still wrapped in his chains. The women all turned and looked too. He was staring straight ahead and pointedly not looking as his not-so-loyal followers filed out of the hall.

I waggled my fingers and the chains disappeared.

Brent stood up, and for a moment I thought he was going to come after me. Then Millicent started to clap, a slow clap. Gradually all the women in the hall joined in. It was the most polite rejection I'd ever heard – and the most effective. Brent grabbed his plans from the white board, he stalked towards the front of the hall and disappeared through the door that led to the church. Deep in the depths of the building we heard a door slam.

I turned to the women.

'Thanks, ladies,' I said. Then I looked at Harry, Chloë and Nell. 'Let's go.'

'I've got my car,' said a voice. It was Millicent. 'Let me drive you home.'

I shook my head, but Harry took Millicent's hand.

'Thank you,' she said.

Chapter 47

When we reached the house, everything was still. Overhead, a dark cloud hovered and rain was beginning to fall. Shadows loomed and the feeling of hopelessness remained.

Harry opened the door with a wave of her hand, and Nell and I followed her inside with Millicent trailing behind. We found Eva and Mum loitering in the hall.

'It feels better already,' Mum whispered. 'How on earth did you manage that?'

I shrugged.

'They kind of did it themselves,' I admitted. 'Millicent helped. How's Suky?'

'No different,' said Mum. 'Jamie took her up to her room. He's with her now.'

'What did you tell him?'

Mum looked at Eva.

'Not much,' they said in unison.

'We just said she'd overdone it,' Eva added.

I almost laughed. Almost.

'Did he buy it?'

'Not sure,' Mum looked thoughtful. 'He just wanted to check on Suky.'

Eva clapped her hands and guided Harry, who looked shell-shocked, towards me. I took her hand and she gripped my fingers tightly.

'Let's get on then,' Eva said purposefully. She took Chloë's hand and Chloë picked up Harry's.

'What should I do?' Millicent asked. She looked scared but exhilarated.

'Ah, join in,' said Mum. 'The more the merrier.'

I kept hold of Harry, then took Nell's hand. Millicent squeezed in between Eva and Mum and smiled at me. There was a feeling of expectation in the air, despite the rain and the horrible oppressive atmosphere.

'Right, ladies,' said Eva. 'All we need you to do is listen.'

Quietly, she and Mum started chanting the words from the horrible skin book. I tried really hard to hear what they were saying, but although I was listening, the actual words seemed to slide away from me. I could feel them though, deep inside. Like the vibration when you're inside a building in London and a tube train goes past underground.

The shadows around us all gathered together, sliding up over the ground. Even I, who had grown up with magic, was terrified, so heaven knows what Chloë, Nell and Millicent were thinking. They didn't move. They just hung on to each other's hands. The shadows slunk up the walls of the house and loomed, like clouds, over our heads.

Mum and Eva kept chanting. Suddenly I was surrounded by shadows and inside them, like I was watching a dream, I could see pictures. I saw my dad, lying bleeding on the dusty ground while soldiers shouted around him. I saw my mum, crying as she waved me off to live with Dad. I saw myself, humiliated, after a boy I slept with at university blanked me the next day in a lecture. And Rebecca, sitting alone in her house, looking at a text message from Dom. I even saw a teenage Jamie, confused and hurt, after I left.

Tears were rolling down my cheeks and I had to clamp my mouth shut to prevent myself shouting at Mum to stop.

Around me, Chloë was crying too, big gasping sobs. Tears were pouring down Harry's face and the scars on Nell's skinny arms glowed red with blood. But no one moved. I was amazed by how brave they were.

Then, suddenly, the shadows disappeared, the sky lightened and the rain stopped. Mum and Eva stopped talking and smiled at each other.

'That's it,' Mum said. 'We've done it.'

I had no idea what had happened, but I could feel that it was good. I grinned at Harry and she grinned back.

A creak on the stairs made us all drop hands.

'Guys?' Jamie popped his head over the bannister, clearly intrigued about what we were up to.

'Erm, Suky's awake and she's asking for you.'

Mum and Eva gave each other a small smile and, each putting an arm round Harry, they went upstairs to see Suky. From nowhere, Allan appeared, a bottle of wine in each hand.

'I knew something big was happening,' he said in his gruff Yorkshire accent. 'So I thought I'd stay out of the way until it was over.'

He opened one of the bottles with a flourish and I got some glasses out of the cupboard.

'Everything OK, is it?'

'I think so,' I said. I handed a large glass of wine to Chloë, then a smaller one to Nell.

Desperate for some space to get my head round what had happened, I poured myself some wine and sneaked off down the garden. Ignoring the raindrops, I sat on a wet garden bench and looked back up at the house. The moon had come out, and I could see the women, our amazing, bold, brave friends, milling about, chatting and laughing. More people were streaming up the hill and I guessed they were all coming to see how Suky was, drawn by the drama of the meeting and the energy of the magic. I could see Nell and Chloë dancing to music that I couldn't even hear and there was a buzz of chatter. In the light of Suky's bedroom window, I could see Harry's silhouette. She was gesturing wildly and I guessed she was giving her mum a hard time for messing with magic that was too powerful for witches like us.

'Budge up.' Jamie plonked himself down next to me.

I smiled at him and he clinked his drink against my now empty glass.

'Top up?' he asked, producing a bottle from behind his back.

'Ooh well done that man,' I said, laughing.

He slopped wine into my glass and I drank.

There was a pause.

'You left your bedroom door open,' he said, trying to sound offhand. 'I noticed you've been packing.'

I nodded.

'I have to go back to London,' I said, hating the expression on his face.

'Back to your boyfriend?'

'No! We're not together now. I just have a life there.' I paused.

'So that's that,' he said.

There was so much to say that I didn't know where to begin. Instead, I just put my hand on his.

'Sorry,' I whispered.

We sat there, hand in hand for a moment, watching the people around the house.

'Anyway,' Jamie began. 'What just happened?'

I shook my head.

'You wouldn't believe me if I told you,' I said.

'Try me.'

I closed my eyes.

'I can't.'

There was a sigh.

'That's always been our problem, Esme,' he said. 'You won't

tell me anything. You won't open up. How can we have a future together if you won't be honest?'

I felt him stand up but I couldn't open my eyes – I didn't want to see him walk away.

'Something happened here tonight,' he said. 'Just like something happened ten years ago. And if you can't tell me what that is, then I don't want to be with you.'

I heard him crunching across the frozen grass, and when I opened my eyes again, he was gone. I caught a brief glimpse of him skirting the side of the house, then I heard his car start.

'That's that,' I said.

Chapter 48

Suky was brilliant. Really. I mean, obviously she wasn't cured, but she was better than she'd been for ages.

'I'm sorry,' she said, when I went in to say goodbye to her. 'I just couldn't face the idea of my radiotherapy dragging on and on, and I thought I could do something about it. It wasn't Harry's fault. She was researching good voodoo. I just twisted her ideas and used them for my own spells.'

I hugged her tightly.

'I'll be back soon,' I said. 'Don't do anything stupid while I'm away.'

I went into my room and started putting the last few bits into my case. I was sorry to go, but I knew it was the right thing to do. I did have one regret, though – Jamie.

Reaching into my drawer I found the photo from years ago. I sat on my Take That bed and gazed at it.

'You're an idiot, Esme.' Chloë was standing in the doorway.

I smiled sadly at her.

'I know,' I said. Chloë sat down next to me and put her arm round me.

'Do you love him?'

'I'm not sure.' I played with a bit of fluff on Jason Orange's nose. 'I think I could.'

'So what are you waiting for?'

'How can I build a life with someone when my life is so . . .' I couldn't think of a word. 'So . . .'

'Unconventional?' Chloë said. 'So bloody what?'

I sighed dramatically.

'I'm a witch, Chlo.'

'What's your point?' Chloë could be very annoying when she wanted to be.

'My point is, most normal people aren't witches.'

'Most normal people can't bite their own toenails,' said Chloë.

'Yeuch,' I said. 'Who does that?'

'Rob!' she said, obviously proud of her husband's talent.

'That's not the same thing,' I said sulkily.

'Tis,' she said. 'What about Allan's love of Doris Day films?'

'Allan does not love Doris Day.'

'He does. Ask him. He knows *Calamity Jane* off by heart.'

I chuckled, despite myself.

'And Nell told me her dad dries himself with a hairdryer when he gets out of the bath,' Chloë said, snorting with laughter. 'He reckons towels are unhygienic.'

'Nooo!' I giggled.

Chloë was almost bouncing on the bed with excitement.

'And!' she said gleefully. 'And! Jamie has Marmite and marmalade on the same piece of toast for breakfast.'

That was, in fact, true. And pretty weird. I looked at Chloë.

'My point, lovely Ez,' she said. 'Is that no one is normal. And thank goodness! Think how bloody boring it'd be if we were.'

I nodded slowly, suddenly realising she was talking sense.

'If Jamie loves you, really loves you, he won't care what you are. He loves you because you're unconventional, not in spite of it.'

I stood up.

'I have to go,' I announced.

'Yeah, you do!' Chloë was triumphant. 'He's on the beach, by the way. I saw him earlier.'

I kissed her on the forehead.

'You are a marvel!' And I headed for the door.

Jamie wasn't in the cave, but he was sitting on the beach, looking out over the water.

I sat down next to him and stared out at the loch.

'I'm coming back you know,' I said.

'In ten years?' he said grouchily.

'Nope. In a month. Maybe six weeks at a push,' I sneaked a sideways look at him. 'I'll see how long it takes to find a tenant for my flat . . .'

He turned his head to look at me.

'I'm coming back,' I repeated. 'For good.'

A smile was spreading across his face.

'I've got a job. Well, it's a transfer really. Same firm, but in Edinburgh. I expect it'll probably be more divorces than celebrity adoptions but that's fine.'

Jamie shook his head, but he was still smiling.

'You're something, you know that? When did you sort that out?'

I waved my hand.

'Oh in a spare moment,' I grinned at him. 'It was Harry's idea, would you believe? She found the job ad, and kind of talked me into it. I did the rest – with a bit of help from my boss, Maggie.' I wrinkled my nose up. 'I've got to do a bit more work so I can practise in Scotland, but it won't take long. I'm a geek, remember, I love studying so . . .'

Jamie kissed me. And this time I kissed him back. And it was just as I remembered and yet so new and exciting.

We kissed for a long time. My lips felt bruised and swollen as we walked hand in hand back up the hill to the house, but I couldn't stop smiling. And yet, there was still one tiny thing I hadn't mentioned.

As we got near home, I thought about what Chloë had said about Jamie loving me whatever I was.

I pulled his arm and stopped walking. He turned to face me, his hair blowing in the wind.

'No more lies,' I said. 'No more half-truths and made-up stories?'

Jamie looked dubious.

'No,' he said firmly. 'None of those. Just us, being upfront and honest with each other.'

'No dramas?' I said. 'And absolutely no freaking out?'

'What?' he said. There was the tiniest amount of fear in his eyes. 'What is it, Ez? You're scaring me.'

I looked at him and thought if our situations were reversed, and he told me he was a wizard, I'd still love him.

I gave him a wonky smile.

'Erm,' I began. 'There's something I need to tell you . . .'

Acknowledgments

Thank you to my parents for giving me a love of books, and to Anna and Nicky for being so excited; I'm excited too! A big hug to Gerda, who has known Esme almost as long as I have; thank you for your constant encouragement and excellent advice. And to Darren, Tom and Sam – I love you very much. You're awesome.

Dear Reader,

We hope you enjoyed reading this book. If you did, we'd be so appreciative if you left a review. It really helps us and the author to bring more books like this to you.

Here at HQ Digital we are dedicated to publishing fiction that will keep you turning the pages into the early hours. Don't want to miss a thing? To find out more about our books, promotions, discover exclusive content and enter competitions you can keep in touch in the following ways:

JOIN OUR COMMUNITY:
Sign up to our new email newsletter: http://smarturl.it/SignUpHQ
Read our new blog www.hqstories.co.uk

🐦 https://twitter.com/HQStories
📘 www.facebook.com/HQStories

BUDDING WRITER?
We're also looking for authors to join the HQ Digital family!
Find out more here:

https://www.hqstories.co.uk/want-to-write-for-us/

Thanks for reading, from the HQ Digital team